A Very Private Performance

Also by Fran Grace
BRANIGAN'S DOG

A Very Private Performance ★

★ ★ by Fran Grace

BRADBURY PRESS ★ SCARSDALE, N.Y.

Bradbury Press, Inc.
2 Overhill Road
Scarsdale, N.Y. 10583
An affiliate of Macmillan, Inc.
Collier Macmillan Canada, Inc.
Manufactured in the United States of America
10 9 8 7 6 5 4 3 2 1
The text of this book is set in 11pt. Times Roman.
Library of Congress Cataloging in Publication Data
Grace, Fran.
A very private performance.
Summary: A self-promoting and ambitious mime and campus cut-up learns about
real talent from those who have it and those close to it.
[1. School stories.   2. Friendship—Fiction]
[Title.
PZ7.G7514Ve   1983   [Fic]   83-6378
ISBN 0-02-736650-2

TO JACK
Look, how thy ring
encompasseth my finger, etc.
As they say,
in Shakespeare

A Very Private Performance

*A*nd now, *live from Houston, Texas, "Celebrity on the Spot" brings you a backstage interview with the sensational young prodigy, Burke Lindstrom. Miss Lindstrom just minutes ago completed her performance as violin soloist with the Houston Symphony Orchestra, playing the technically demanding Concerto in D Minor by Sibelius. She is being interviewed by Abraham Aaronson, music critic emeritus for the* Los Angeles Times *and special commentator for this television network. Mr. Aaronson.*

—Thank you. Burke and I have been talking about a mishap at the outset of tonight's stellar performance. She appeared to trip, but caught herself . . .

—It couldn't have happened at a worse time—at my entrance, after all my preconcert psyching up! Of course I was showing off, so it was my own fault, I suppose.

—In what way were you showing off, Burke? You appeared to be simply walking on stage from the wings, when something tripped you . . .

—I was wearing high heels, which I'm not used to, and I'm afraid I was flaunting this new concert gown—I had picked it out myself. The problem is, it's a bit too long—I chose it at the last minute . . .

—It's—er—a different *approach from the child prodigy in demure white that we Burke Lindstrom fans are all used to. Let's back up camera number three, there, for a medium-long shot, so our television audience can see the* new *Miss Lindstrom, full length. The effect is quite—er— sophisticated.*

—I'm sixteen, Mr. Aaronson. It's time I took responsibility for my personal wardrobe—as well as for my pratfalls!

—Well, happily, you didn't take a fall, and we're all relieved. You've kept your cool most remarkably, Burke, considering the magnitude of tonight's concert, and the fact that this interview on "Celebrity on the Spot" is your very first encounter with the media, after all these insular years. Can you share the secret of your composure?

—Yes. A great weight has been lifted off me.

—Will you explain?

—Perhaps not to your satisfaction, Mr. Aaronson. It has to do with Mira Vista High School—in Belview Beach. About my choosing to go there.

—Is there someone special—at Mira Vista High School?

—Yes, of course.

★ ★ *1*

She looked like a space case. I noticed something different about her the minute I dashed into room 131 for my new spring semester junior English Lit. class, sweating and panting and nearly late. I'd bumped into my running buddy, Roberto (Rabbit) Rodriguez, between classes, and he'd bet me a Paco's taco he could beat me in an 880 right then on the track, since we'd both missed our usual preschool workout. I circled the track twice in 2:20. I'd be buying.

As I headed for the only seat left in the room, I did a double take—this pinch-faced, purple-eyed girl had a hank of red hair matching my own. She was dressed all in white in something ruffled and Victorian straight out of a nine-teenth-century *Godey's Lady's Book* (I'm into collecting old magazines). She sat stiff and still, a snow cone with a glob of strawberry topping.

I looked across the room at my girl, Justine Landry. What a difference! Justine's a foxy Cajun—"that means Acadian, *cher*, like Injun is Indian"—with the smarts, an eyeful in tight jeans and message T's and a head not ex-actly stuffed with sawdust. We had met in the Maskers, the club for "actors and others" at Mira Vista High. She said she was born in a log cabin in the Louisiana swamps. I bought that—could she ever sing those Cajun songs, like

"Madeleine," and play the guitar as sweet and dark as Mississippi Mud Cake.

I tore my eyes away from her and bestowed my friendly-perfunctory nod on the Snow Cone, the nod I usually reserve for New People. It can't be too perfunctory—the New People may turn out to be friends. And it can't be too friendly—I may end up hating them.

"Hi," I said, as I passed her and sat down behind her. Obviously she wasn't beach people. In Belview Beach, the tanning capital of the world, or at least of Southern California, most redheads take their chances with the sun. Freckles are in. Mine are running together in a really good tan. Her face was plain frozen yogurt.

She didn't say anything. She didn't even nod. I didn't think I was going to like her.

The seating chart came by, and she handed it back to me, hardly turning around. I looked at her name: "Burke Lindstrom," in seat number three, row number five. Burke! Weird. I squeezed my name into number four, row number five. Maximilian Murphy. Someday, the whole thing would go up in lights at the Music Center (a figure of speech—they use billboards). MAXIMILIAN MERRIWETHER MURPHY IN AN EVENING OF MIME! *Not* Max Murphy—*that* had the sound of a two-bit hoofer in a traveling medicine show.

The seating chart got back to Mr. Nielson, but he didn't look at it when he said, "We are pleased to have a well-known young violinist in our midst. She's new to our school, and I hope you'll make her feel welcome. Burke Lindstrom." He gestured, smiling, towards the Snow Cone. "I myself have heard her play at the Music Center. Welcome, Burke."

The Music Center! Burke Lindstrom—in lights at the Music Center? I instantly hated her.

This flake in front of me says, smooth as soft ice cream and just as cold, "You are very kind. Thank you, Mr. Nielson. I am sure I will be very happy here with my peers at Mira Vista High School." Peers! I couldn't see if she smiled or not. She sounded dead serious.

After class I waited until she'd left the room before I even got up from my seat. Naturally Justine hung around, too. Love-in time. It seemed like forever before everyone else had gone, and Mr. Nielson finally got his books and clipboards together and started for the door. He tossed back, deadpanning, "I'm glad to see my class is so popular that you two can't bear to leave." He left the door open. I waited a beat and shut it, even though a closed door is just a challenge to the inquiring minds of M. V. High.

Of course I wasted no time in wrapping my arms around Justine and indulging in a long, soft kiss. With a schedule like mine, you've got to move fast. I had to bend way down from my nearly six feet two to her mere five four, but believe me it was a no-sweat chore. She was all warm curves and soft lips.

"No feelies, Maximilian, you!" She pushed me away with her usual virgin verve, but her big dark eyes were laughing up at me. "But lookies are okay, yes? Do you see what I say, Maximilian?" She pulled back so that I could read the message across the two sacred bulges: *J'aime Jambalaya.*

I'm not into French. A mime doesn't need language. "Jamie Jamba-lay-a," I sounded out, suspiciously. "Who's he, some Cajun cat down home in Houma?" Houma is Justine's home town, somewhere down around New Orleans, and to hear her tell it, it's a paradise on earth, a sort of mini-Paris in the marsh.

She laughed. "Maximilian, you are a yo-yo, you!" She

had picked up on California-speak pretty well for being here just a year, since coming to live with her Aunt Celeste (a nice enough lady-engineer type, but too much into women's rights for my taste). It seems Justine's *tante* didn't want her only niece growing up rough-and-ready with nine rowdy brothers, shucking oysters and skinning muskrats along the banks of the bayous.

"Stop laughing," I ordered. "I'm not with you, Lily Tomlin."

She wound down. "It just says, 'I love jambalaya.' That's rice and shrimps and oysters and onions and Tabasco . . ." The spell was broken. She added hurriedly, "I am going now to the cafeteria, *cher*—for a burrito." She flung her bookbag over one shoulder.

I caught her by her hair. It was easy to do—she wore it down to her waist, thick and dark and wavy. I reeled her in—but missed a kiss when she said firmly, "Oh, Maximilian, we must hurry! The High Noon Show, it is time, yes?"

I let her go. Judging by the number of burritos (laced with Tabasco) she chonked down, she'd be ten minutes late in reporting to the brown-bagger benches as it was. Even though the show was my idea, my personal forum, my own sneak preview of gigs I planned to use when I went pro, I had to admit it was the beautiful Belle of the Bayou who frequently kept the lunch bunch from changing channels.

I hurried out the door, concentrating on the Red Riding Hood pantomime I'd be rehearsing today for the next Inner-City Playhouse show—I was a once-a-month volunteer with the recreation department's program for disadvantaged kids.

When I hit the main walk to the quad, I really hit it. I

found myself airborne, then thrown sideways, my head luckily landing on the lawn, my books scudding everywhere.

"You clumsy klutz, Trinka Teitelbaum!" I rose gingerly to my knees. She teetered back and forth on her fat wheels, laughing down at me. "Skating on campus is illegal! I'll sue the pants off you!"

She laughed so hard her center of gravity shifted and she nearly crashed beside me. When she got control again she said, "What pants?" She was wearing her usual winterized roller skating outfit, a fake-fur bikini (this one was leopard) with matching knee pads and leg warmers.

"Just wait'll you get caught, T Squared! You'll wish you *did* have pants, tough ones! Forty lashes are too good for you!"

"They'll have to catch me first! Hey, Maxie, did you know your ears are as red as your hair?" She raced away at top speed, then went into a long, gliding arabesque, one leg sticking straight out behind her. I shook my fist after her as I feebly gathered up my books.

I decided to forgo the lawsuit in favor of beating Justine to the opening act. *I* was the M.C. My injuries luckily receded as I went from a limp to a lope to a gallop. When I arrived at the picnic pavilion, the stage was all mine. The brown-baggers had moved the benches into the sun, avoiding the shade of the green corrugated awning, this being February. I was greeted by the usual splatter of applause and mock cheers, followed by a few alarming sniggers, then an unexpected burst of laughter.

I was about to acknowledge my public, arms outstretched, when I caught a glimpse of my right elbow poking through my long-sleeved T (and Mom had just sewed up that hole a couple of days ago). The comfortable broken-in knees of my favorite jeans had broken out under the Teitelbaum onslaught, and the whole outfit was smeared randomly with green grass stains. I looked more like Chaplin's Little Tramp grown large and loutish than the smooth Shields and Yarnell type my audience had come to expect.

Then I saw *her,* the ultimate contrast: prim, pure, and pristine, sitting in the first row. Burke Lindstrom. If Trinka had thrown my timing off a little, I knew the Snow Cone was going to throw it off a lot. Timing is half the art for a mime. I couldn't keep my eyes off her. Instead of a paper sack, she was eating out of a small white wicker basket. I tried to catch the Menu for Today—hummingbird eggs and French-dipped butterfly wings? Her frozen blueberry eyes stared back at me.

For the first time in my two-year career, I felt unnerved, as they say. Red Riding Hood wouldn't cut it today. I couldn't think of another act, out of all those I had practiced in front of my closet-door mirror. So I went into my old reliable, the walking-in-place routine, always an attention-getter. People can't figure out how you do it, walking so fast and never getting anywhere; just like life, Justine says. It's easy—you do it by sliding back for every step forward. But nobody notices the slide.

I fished in my pocket for my mime mask—I almost always have it with me. From a distance you can hardly tell it from real clown-white, and it's instant make-up. When I stretched my mouth into the biggest, widest, tallest, toothiest grin this side of Marcel Marceau, the great French mime, I had the kids with me, stomping and calling, "Way to go!"

I caught a glimpse of Burke. She was wiping her fingers on what looked like a real napkin, the kind the Murphys save for Thanksgiving. Her fingers were long and thin and pale—about what you'd expect of a long, thin, and pale violinist. A violinist—instant inspiration!

I clown-walked over to Burke and pretended to borrow her basket. The Snow Cone's thermostat was stuck on freeze and she didn't even react. Back on stage, I went on walking in place, but this time I was "carrying" the basket. I mimed its size with my hands. This big guy, six feet two almost, toting Burke's mouse-house, was pulling a lot of laughs. Then I stopped walking and made a big thing of opening the tiny basket. I let my eyebrows shoot up (surprise) and my head click forward (curiosity). At last I took out an (invisible) king-size violin. It was so "heavy" I could hardly hoist it up under my chin. I started "playing," swooping, bobbing, and weaving like a frenetic fiddler in an old silent movie—shot at sixteen frames a second and running at twenty-four.

The audience concentrated on my scenario. You could have heard a Twinkie crumble. The "solo" suddenly ended with imaginary brickbats and boos from the stands, in which I gave one of my best tragic-clown satirical interpretations. Sadly, I "braced" the giant imaginary fiddle against my knee and stuck my nose proudly in the air. I was the ex-great concert artist reduced to playing a country hoedown! I was pretty pleased with the way the improvisation was going. I ended it by "stuffing" the big instrument back into its little wicker case, then spread my arms wide, inviting applause.

What I got instead was a bag of popcorn smack in the face. Shocked, I saw that the popcorn-pitcher was my own cute Cajun, standing near Burke in the front row, feet apart, hands on hips—glowering.

"Hey, now—just a . . ." I began, torn between consternation and indignation, as I riffled my hair, brushing out a shower of the buttery stuff.

"Maximilian, that was not very nice!" came sharply from Justine's direction, over the ripple of laughter from the stands.

Before I could will my mouth closed—it had dropped open in shock—I was bumped aside by a fast hip and a sharp elbow.

"She is so *new*, her! For shame on you!" my Louisiana lovely stage-whispered, taking charge. She was wearing her guitar slung over the left sholder on a black hand-crocheted strap with pink roses. She swung her arms out, graciously acknowledging scattered cheers, and giving me the *coup de grâce* with a half a burrito in the face, a slapstick act even the legendary Three Stooges would have envied. I ripped off my white mime mask, bloodied by chunky taco sauce, and swiped at the refries and lumps of soft tortilla sticking to my chin.

"Hey, what d'you think you're . . ." I sputtered.

She interrupted. "An accident, *cher*. Look, you made her cry, you!"

I glanced at the Snow Cone, sitting hunched over her basket. "Hey, but I didn't mean to . . ." But did I? I rushed over to her. "Hey, Burke, it was only a . . ." I impulsively reached out to her, putting a hand on her arm.

She jumped to her feet, screaming. She screamed and screamed, and as the white blur raced past me, I caught the high-pitched shriek, "You touched me! You touched me!"

I stood there staring at my leprous hands, mottled with taco sauce, as the hoarse warning buzzer sounded over the fading cry, "You touched me!"

★ ★ 2

All afternoon I exerted my most powerful Thought Control, hoping Burke Lindstrom had disappeared forever from my life. But when she showed up in my sixth period History of European Civilization, I knew my Thought Control needed more work. Her face was clown-white as she turned away from me. I took a seat on the opposite side of the room from her.

Mrs. Hodges didn't pay any attention to the Snow Cone at first, not until roll call. When she got to the Music Center star, she paused. "Burke Lindstrom. Is he here?" Burke raised her hand. "You're Burke Lindstrom?" Mrs. H said crossly, as though that was Burke's big mistake, just being Burke Lindstrom. I had to agree with her. "I never would have guessed Burke Lindstrom was a girl," she went on peevishly. "I do wish parents would consider the consequences of these ridiculous given names. They can be a lifelong liability." She glanced at Burke disapprovingly, and I could see the Music Center star was off to a slow start with Mrs. H. It was pretty gratifying.

Burke didn't deign to reply. She held her head high, nose in the air, and stared straight ahead, like a queen rising above the commoners.

I had planned on avoiding Burke, any way possible,

when class was over. But she cornered me outside the door. She was very direct. I found out she was *always* very direct.

"Why did you find it necessary to disparage me? I doubt if you have ever seen me perform. I'd be surprised if you've ever seen *any* violinist perform, judging from your act—except perhaps a country fiddler. You did *that* rather well." Her eyes sank into mine like raisins in Mom's custard pie.

"Well, hey, why'd *you* find it necessary to scream like a plucked peacock?" I demanded, annoyed. "It was just a slight case of taco sauce, not rape!"

"Taco sauce?" She looked baffled. "Maximilian, you *touched* me. Please don't *ever* do it again."

"Don't worry," I snapped, grinding my teeth. She wasn't exactly my idea of a sex symbol.

"It was a shock, on top of your poor performance."

Apologizing was the farthest thing from my mind. So I was disgusted to hear myself mumbling, "I—usually practice my acts in front of my mirror at home, first. But this was—just an extemporaneous thing, like a street interaction. Mimes do it all the time. Nobody takes it seriously." So why the humble mumble, Maximilian Merriwether Murphy?

"I did. Everybody did. You should know. You had the very *best* mirror—the audience. In another minute they'd have given you the hook, if that girl hadn't." She paused, while I fought for control, my Adam's apple bobbing up and down. Then she took me by surprise. "What do you mean, 'street interaction'?"

She had pulled the right strings. I began dancing at the end of them. "Street interaction is when a street mime draws someone nearby into his act."

"To make a fool of her?" She was watching me.

I stood my ground. "Not on purpose. The mime just wants the audience to relate to the action, that's all. Street interaction pulls the audience right into the fantasy. Miming's a lot like music, you know—my instrument's the body, yours is a fiddle. You practice scales every day, I practice isolations—moving each part of the body separately without moving the rest. You wouldn't run all your notes together, would you?"

"Maximilian, you sound *serious* about mime! I thought—you were just—having fun by making fun of *me*, out there today."

I couldn't resist. "Just fiddling around, hah?" I started to walk away. After all, I didn't want the whole student body to see me buddying up to the Snow Cone. *"Ciao,"* I tossed over my shoulder, picking up speed as I crossed the campus. I could hear her trying to keep up, behind me.

"Maximilian, wait! I'd like to hear more about . . ."

The traffic circle was all clear and I started to cross it when I was jerked to a stop. Burke had grabbed my arm. Before I could snatch it back she dropped it like a hot briquette at a barbecue. I whirled and took a look at her, and stared in surprise. She seemed to be trying to say something, her mouth working soundlessly. She looked like a puppet in search of a puppeteer. She scared me.

"Hey," I said. "Easy. Everything's cool."

She got her voice back, but it came out small and tight. "I—I'm *sorry,* Maximilian. I didn't mean to—touch you, it's just that . . ."

"Hey, hey, when did I say *I'm* an untouchable?"

She was whiter than yogurt. "It's just that—just that— *Father* isn't here!" She was looking wildly around. "He planned to—pick me up!"

"Hold on. Are you sure he was supposed to be here? Most fathers aren't off work at three-fifteen. Mine doesn't get off until five."

"My father's a banker! It's easy for him to leave work at three. He *promised* he'd be here! I don't even know the way home from here. It's *miles* away!"

"No problem," I said without thinking, which is one of *my* problems. "Belview Beach isn't all that big, just five square miles. Tell me where you live, and I'll point you in the right direction."

"I'd—better wait a few more minutes. But don't leave me! Stay here!"

Stay here, on exhibition with the Snow Cone? At the busiest crossroads on campus? "Well—ah," I stumbled— then I remembered the meeting. "I've got a meeting at three-thirty, the Maskers. It's our first for the spring semester. We're working out for Arbor Day."

Her eyebrows shot up. "Do you mean you celebrate *Arbor Day* at this school?"

"So what did you celebrate at *your* old school?" I noticed she'd dyed her eyebrows brown. Mine are as red as my hair. Hers looked funny.

"I have never been to public school before." Her nose was starting to tilt.

"So what did you celebrate in your *private* school?" I tried not to sneer.

"I have always been tutored."

I looked at her. "Tutored! Well, now! How come you're slumming at M.V. High, if that isn't too personal a question?"

"Not at all. I wanted to come. To be with my peers."

I stared at her. "Run that by me again, sometime." I looked at my Thrifty Drug Store watch. "Hey! *My* peers are going to lock me out if I don't get to Maskers on the double." One peer, especially. I took a step towards the curb.

"Maximilian! Wait!" She had stepped in front of me. Her eyes looked the way the little raccoon's did when Dad and I rescued him from a corner of the garage, where he had trapped himself. I hadn't seen the little robber in years—Belview Beach's wildlife must be extinct. . . .

I was grabbed by the shirttail. "What you are doing, Maximilian? Where you are going? There is Maskers, yes?"

My voice came out several decibels louder than I expected. "Oh, it's you—Justine!"

Burke cut in, throwing the fat in the fire, "He's going home with me. I don't know the way."

Justine's big brown eyes turned into little slits. "So, Maximilian, you are going home with *her*." She turned contemplative. "You have heard of gris-gris, yes?"

"Gree-gree?" I'd never heard of it.

"A spell. A Cajun spell. I am thinking a gris-gris, maybe, will be put on you, *cher*." Her voice was dark and full of foreboding.

Burke said impatiently, "We'd better go. Father must have forgotten, and I still have four more hours of practicing today."

"Maximilian, I have at home one chunk of red hair." Justine smiled secretly. "*Your* red hair. And one can easily find a toad, yes? One dried toad."

"What are you talking about? Dried toads! Maximilian, come on!" Burke started to snatch at my arm, but pulled back as though my torn sleeve had scorched her hand.

I glanced from one to the other of them. Then I hit on

a solution. "Why not come with us, Cherie? It's a great day for a fast walk." The air was clear and crisp, and with Justine along this might be an okay gig. I decided I'd better find out the extent of my offer. "Say, where do you live, Burke?" She gave an address on the Strand—the North End, the swinging end. I couldn't picture it, the Snow Cone among the beach girls of the golden thighs and undressed eyes.

Justine looked at me thoughtfully. "But three is *not* company, yes?" She smiled mysteriously—Mona Lisa. "I will not forget the gris-gris, me." A chunk of *my* hair? No way. She walked away, blue-jeaned hips swinging beneath a pink nylon ski jacket.

My eyes followed her as I said quickly, "Listen, Burke, you go west on Belview Beach Boulevard until you hit the Strand on the beach. And then you walk north until you find your house. You don't need anyone with you. It's simple."

"No! Father wouldn't approve! I'm *not* to go wandering around by myself. It isn't safe! Please, Maximilian . . ." Her animal eyes got to me. Scared.

"Okay, okay. Come on." Face it, Maximilian Merriwether Murphy: you're one of those suckers Barnum catalogued.

We took the route I had told her about. I wasn't in my best mood, and I set a fast pace. I could hear her behind me, panting.

"Please, Maximilian—you walk *very* fast."

"I'm in training for the marathon," I snapped. As a matter of fact, I was.

"The marathon? Good heavens! That's twenty-five miles, I think." She came puffing up beside me. "Are you kidding?"

"No. Twenty-six miles, three hundred eighty-five yards. I'm pointing towards the 1988 Olympics."

"Really? You really do run twenty-six miles now?"

"Not yet. I still hit the wall at twenty-two miles." I was getting into it. "But I'll be ready by 1988." With the Rabbit running with me, I couldn't miss. He was on the cross-country and track teams, a great distance runner. I wasn't a team jock, but I went to the meets as often as I could, just to cheer the Rabbit on. He was half Tarahumara Indian, he said, from the famous tribe of runners in the Sierra Occidental of northern Mexico. He was also an illegal alien, which hardly anybody knew but me, and I wasn't telling.

"But you said you're a mime. Where does all that running fit in?" She wasn't puffing now. I had let her catch up.

"Does it have to fit in? Don't you do anything besides fiddle?" She shook her head. I might have guessed. What a ding-a-ling. I said, "Well, okay, so you're famous and probably rich." She didn't deny it, so I went on. "I happen to like those gimmicks too. The marathon won't make me rich. Famous, maybe, but not rich. Mime will make me *both* rich and famous." I had written the whole scenario, but I wasn't telling her—or anybody, right then. All the same, I could almost *feel* Great-Granddad's mythical razor strop on the seat of my pants.

"What!" Dad's voice roared inside my head. "My son a high school drop-out? Take that (*whang*) . . . and THAT (*WHANG*) . . ."

"But Dad," I'd plead, offering up my Certificate of Proficiency, "I'm NOT a drop-out . . ."

". . . and that (*WHANG!*) Then get back to school, drop-out, and earn a *real* diploma!"

I must have been cringing because Burke turned to look

at me, and for the first time I saw a flash of humor in her eyes. I didn't like it. She was laughing at me. Then her gaze swept beyond me.

"Oh—here's Father. Father!"

A dream car out of the twenties or early thirties floated into focus alongside us—long, elegant, pure lines, white and gleaming with burnished brass trim: golden exhaust headers, brass-rimmed "lamps" that were as big as five-dollar pizzas! A golden Flying Lady ornament danced on the hood; two half-ladies perched on the fenders. The distinctive design of the rear of the car could mean only one thing: I was in the presence of that great classic, a Boat-Tail Auburn!

Burke had opened the door and was tilting the bucket seat forward. "I said, get in, Maximilian."

I climbed into the back, sitting down on the butter-soft white leather bench-seat while remembering my "Pleased-to-meet-you-sir" bit. Mr. Lindstrom asked for my address and I gave it automatically, 1251 Ocean View Drive, as I ogled the hand-rubbed wooden dashboard up front, and what looked like a soft-sheened oak steering wheel. I sucked in my breath.

"Wow!" I breathed. I didn't think anyone heard me. I wished the white top was pushed back; I'd never ridden in a real convertible before.

"You like it, Maximilian?" Mr. Lindstrom asked.

"It's great! How old is it, anyway? Nineteen twenties?" I felt a stab of guilt. I shouldn't even be here, enjoying myself. I should be jogging back to the Maskers meeting, where Justine was waiting for me, I hoped. I was a sucker for a super car. Then I thought of the little yellow bug I was slaving my life away for, working Friday and Saturday swing shifts at Sam's Super Service. Wheels. I lusted after wheels.

"How old? About three years. I built it," Mr. Lindstrom said.

"You *built* it?" It was early thirties, at the latest.

Burke said, "From a kit. Father built it from a customizing kit. He's *very* clever." I noticed the Mutual Admiration Society, as Mom says, up front, as they turned to smile at each other.

"It must be worth a pirate's poke," I said, sucking in my breath at the lavish all-white interior.

"It's worth about sixty thousand as a turnkey model, that is, all put together as is," Mr. Lindstrom said. Sixty thou! "But the kit costs only about nine thousand. This is the extended wheelbase model, a hundred and thirty-two inches."

"Wow!" I was repeating myself.

"Plus two or three thousand for accessories. I had my own chassis, a '69 Ford."

"Wow!" I hated myself, so I added, "It's a class act." The computer in my head was clicking away like Space Invaders. "What could I build on a VW Bug chassis?" But why, I asked myself, would I want to do that? A Bug is a classic all by itself!

"On a VW chassis? Let's see. How about the MG-TD, about 1952? The kit would cost you between five and six thousand dollars."

"Wow." I wished he hadn't added that last. An MG-TD! "Convertible?"

"Right. Leather-grained expanded vinyl top, like this one. Why don't you go to the next Kit Car Show—er, what's your name again, son?"

"Maximilian. Maximilian Murphy—sir. What about the show?"

"There's one coming up at the Convention Center. *Kit Car Magazine* will have the stats. I'll send word through Burke."

"An MG-TD—wow!" I mumbled.

"Oh, yes, Burke," Mr. Lindstrom said, as though suddenly remembering her, "I have a message for you. Lanny will be over tonight."

"Lanny Van Alston! No! I don't want to see him!"

"Now, Burke. Ann-Oliveras called Angelica today, and Angelica called me at the office. I'm just the messenger."

"Father, why didn't Lanny call *me,* instead of having *his* mama call *my* mama, like a kindergartner? No. I *won't* see him! He touches me! I can't stand him!"

"Burke, considering the Van Alstons' generosity, and the fact that I *do* think you want the Guarnerius . . .

"Oh, Father, it's my *dream* instrument! But the Van Alstons do that sort of thing all the time. They're very *proud* of being patrons of the arts."

"They have a special fondness for *you,* Burke. You know that. And they've invested heavily in your career. Can't you please them by seeing Lanny occasionally? You won't find a nicer kid—good family, good manners, good-looking, even a good school. What can you possibly have against him?"

I was the Ghost Rider. They had forgotten me.

"He touches me," she repeated, and I saw her shiver, as though someone had dropped an ice cube down her back. "He's so—proprietary!"

"Turn here, sir," I said, and they both jumped a little. "And thank you for the ride."

Mr. Lindstrom nodded, but nobody said a word until I

had climbed out of the Auburn. I closed the door after Burke had stepped back in, and started towards our picket gate. I wasn't quite out of earshot, though, when I heard her father say, "Don't make friends too fast, Burke. That boy seems very—ordinary."

I turned, planning a clean but cutting one-liner, when the Auburn glided away. So I pushed open the gate and stomped along the redwood rounds towards our clapboard house. Suddenly I had to laugh. Not to worry, Father Lindstrom! That freak with the frozen soul—make friends fast? I sent out a strong ESP to Lanny what's-his-name to go over to Burke's house and *touch* her tonight.

I got my bike and pedaled back to school on the double. There was a full house at the Maskers meeting, but my Queen of Hearts was missing.

"She went off with Brad Bedford," Gary, the M.C. pro tem in my absence, called from the stage, seeing me looking anxiously around the room.

"What!" I said, aghast. "The *HUNK?* Not the *Hunk?*" He was the captain of the football team—One Hunk of Man to the girls and a meatball to the guys. "*She* wouldn't do that!"

Doreen, who was on stage reading for Lady Teazle in the Maskers' version of *The School for Scandal,* said, "I saw him hanging around the door, looking at her. And when she got up to leave—zap! Sorry, lover." She was probably only sorry that it wasn't her, instead of Justine.

"Laugh, clown, laugh!" Gary grinned.

★ ★ 3

"My fren, you are, how you say, draggin' your butt," the Rabbit said the next morning. We were running in one of those clammy "low overcasts," Los Angeles weather-talk for drizzle. "My fren, this is the best weather for runnin'! Come on, you never goin' to make the Olympics like this! You never even goin' to make the Kola King Marathon in March!"

"I'm thinking," I said, doggedly plunging along as though I were wearing cement boots instead of the New Balance shoes I'd gotten for Christmas (as light as Mom's lemon chiffon pie). "I'm probably in big trouble with Justine, Rabbit, and believe me, she's in even bigger trouble with me."

"Justine! Forget Justine! Jus' get through this workout, Mox, now, this mornin'!" Forget Justine. The Rabbit had tunnel vision. You want something, you go for it. Rabbit wanted just one thing: to be the world's greatest runner. Well, he was on his way. He was best in the league, probably best in the state, and already college coaches were sniffing at his heels at the big meets. They weren't the only ones nosing around the Rabbit, either. He and his mom managed to stay just one hop ahead of the INS feds— the Immigration and Naturalization Service—by changing addresses about every other week, moving silently within a network of friends and cousins. Somehow the Rabbit always showed up at Mira Vista High School, no matter where he lived, and his mom kept up with her cleaning-lady jobs in the million-dollar mansions on the Strand. "I will beat this rop yet, Mox!" he kept telling me, his wide mouth splitting his dark Indian face with a gleeful smile. I was betting on him.

We met at our lockers. It wasn't accidental. We almost always met at our lockers just before third period. We glared briefly at each other—her cheeks glowed shocking pink, matching her T-shirt. My face felt as red as my hair.

"You . . . !" we both began at the same time, but since I had a louder voice, I got the floor.

"You—went off with *him,* the *Hunk*—you *wench!* I can't trust you!"

"Oh! That is a bad word! *You* are a—a *ouaouaron!* You went *home*—with *her!*"

I recognized the Cajun word—she had called me a bull-frog before, ripe and ready for the pointed stick. But I got in the first jab. "Dead wrong. Her *father* picked us up—and took *me* home. But I biked right back here, and where were you? *Not* at Maskers, where you were supposed to be. Now explain Brad Bedford, *if* you can." I tried to maintain my glare, but I could feel it disintegrating. She was pink spun sugar, and my eyes were devouring her, pique and all.

"But what is there to explain, *cher?*" she shrugged. Miss Innocence! "He went with me to my locker, and I got my guitar, and I went home—*without* him, yes, Maximilian?"

I was immediately suspicious. "How come he let you escape?"

She grinned. "I hit him."

"Oh, no, not *feelies*, Cherie? On the way to your *locker?*"

"He was *looking* feelies, him. So I hit him." She smiled smugly.

"Naturally." I breathed a sigh of relief, as they say. "Good work, Cherie." I reached into my locker and took out a paper sack. "Come on, we'll be late."

I had a somewhat less public place than the hall in mind. So when we got to the big bottle-brush tree on the walk to our Lit. class, I deftly maneuvered her behind it.

"Peace offering." I handed her the paper sack.

She took out the stem of fourteen bright yellow beauties. "Orchids?"

"Right. Cymbidium orchids." The stem was the first from the patio plants in three years. Dad and I had given Mom the original cymbidium plant for a Mother's Day, when it was flaunting four long stems with fifty-six orchids. That effort evidently busted its gut, and even though we'd divided it and repotted, all four plants had drooped dispiritedly ever since, until now. I felt a twinge of guilt, just a twinge.

"Very nice, Maximilian." Justine's smile erased the guilt. "But I have no place to put this, *cher,* thank you just the same. My locker is full of guitar." She pushed the stem back into my hand.

I was dismayed. What a low blow. And Mom would come through with a verbal right hook later. Well, at least I could—ah, return the stem to her, slightly used.

I'd have to activate Plan Two, against my better judgment. I knew this plan still needed polishing—and enameling. But I reached in my pocket anyway and brought out the brass ring I was making in metals class. I took Justine's right hand and slipped it on the middle finger—a perfect fit, of course, as the band was the adjustable type. It looked pretty good "as is." The brass butterfly spread its wings over her index and third fingers, almost seeming to flutter as the sunlight touched it.

"A butterfly ring! Oh, you are sweet, Maximilian, you!" She held up her hand, admiring my work of art.

I swelled with pride, as they say. "You like?" I put my arms around her.

Her smile was an invitation. I promptly kissed her.

"I have news, me," she said breathlessly, when I finally let her come up for air. "I wasn't going to tell you, Maximilian. I was very angry, *cher*. But now I am not." I could see she wasn't. I'd rather have gone along with our mellowing out, but she opted for conversation. "So I will tell you now, *cher*. Maman is inviting you home with me, to Houma, for Christmas."

"That's news?" I looked at her in amazement. "Christmas is ten months away. Forever." I picked up my books and the sack with the orchids.

"Not next Christmas, Maximilian. *This* Christmas. Spring break."

"Justine, Cherie—sort it out. Hey, we better split for Lit., as they say." I started to propel her out from behind the bush but she planted her feet like roots and laughed up at me. I dropped my books and gathered her in, tilting up her chin with one hand. But who can kiss a mouth in perpetual motion?

"Cajuns have Christmas when convenient, them," she chattered. "Like the Landrys, *cher*. When trapping is over—for nutria, and maybe muskrats."

"I guess I'm not reading you," I breathed, my mouth hovering just above hers. "You mean you haven't had Christmas yet? Then what do you call last December twenty-fifth when I gave you a charm bracelet I made myself in woodshop, with little dingles that spelled 'Cherie' . . ."

"And I gave you a belt I crocheted myself, *cher,* with green swamp flowers. That you never wore, hahn?"

"I'm saving it for a guitar strap when you finally get around to teaching me to play." I pressed my mouth firmly against hers—at last. Her eyes closed. I gave my hand permission to sneak under the back of her message T: *"CODOFIL—Non!"* My fingers were edging nicely northward when I felt a sharp cut on the knuckles.

"No feelies, you wump," she murmured dreamily, her eyes closed, her lips smiling—her right hand still clenched.

"That's *wimp,*" I said huskily, drawing her closer.

The warning buzzer sounded, and our Magic Moment disappeared like Mom's marshmallow pie. Reluctantly I retrieved our books and we headed for class.

"Maman said I could bring a friend," Justine continued conversationally. "We will fly."

"Fly? Who's paying?" I'd bet Maman, Papa, and Justine's nine brothers didn't have a "friend" of my gender in mind.

"Tante Celeste pays for me, her. You pay for you, *cher.* Why not? You are rich, Maximilian. There is all that money from your job at the gas station, yes." I thought of us wealthy gas-station attendants, drawing big minimum scale. "And where do you spend it? Not on movies and proms and pizzas on Friday and Saturday nights, Maximilian. I don't think so, hahn?" She watched me, smiling.

I squeezed her hand. "Your Aunt Celeste is saving you from us high-school honchos on the big nights, anyway, Cherie. So you get all that up-scale culture, like ballet and theater, and I save bucks for my VW Bug." It was a classic—canary yellow, a '67 with a rebuilt '71 engine. This guy down the street was asking twenty-nine hundred for that little nugget, but seeing it's me, and he's known me since I rode my Murphy trike up and down the sidewalk past his garage, he's letting it go for twenty-five. I tried to forget the six *thou* price tag on my "pie in the sky," as Dad puts it—the MG-TD.

"But it is not so many—bucks—to go to Houma, *cher.*" Her smile was a strawberry tart, sweet and spicy. "We will fly to Houston, and my brother Albert will drive us to Houma. It is cheaper than flying to New Orleans."

It was cheaper not to go at all. Her fantasy was getting out of hand. "No way, Cherie." I tore my eyes away from her lips. "The bucks are marked money, *ear*marked for the car. I'd have to jog all the way to the bayou." I picked up the pace towards Mr. Nielson's room.

"So, Maximilian," she said as we neared English Lit., her folksinger's voice warm and vibrant and carrying, "You *can* kiss a car, it is possible. But it *cannot kiss back,* yes?"

"Shhh!" I hissed.

"But do not shhhh me, Maximilian, *cher!*" the dulcet tones rang out. "For your next kiss from *me,* you will have to beg, I guarantee!"

A burst of laughter greeted us as we walked in. We were the last to arrive, definitely center stage. I crouched low in my seat, aware that my ears were red flags.

Mr. Nielson glanced up from his roll book. "I'm afraid I must side with Maximilian, in this case, Justine. 'Had

we but world enough, and time,/ This coyness, lady, were
no crime/ . . . The grave's a fine and private place,/ But
none, I think, do there embrace.' Who wrote those lines,
Maximilian, and when?''

I felt the glow on my ears spreading all over my face.
"Ah . . .'' I mumbled, ducking down to stuff the paper
sack with the orchids on the shelf under my seat.

"I'm afraid not,'' Mr. Nielson said. "Volunteers?''

Of course the Snow Cone's hand shot up. The congen-
ital showoff. Mr. Nielson nodded in her direction.
"Burke?''

"Andrew Marvell. Around sixteen fifty. He and Milton
were the only great lyricists of the Puritan period. *To His
Coy Mistress* is the name of the poem. The two octosyl-
labic couplets quoted were from two different verses.''

The whole class stared at her. I felt my eyes boring
straight through her, then I did a double take. She looked
different. The ruffles were gone. She was wearing a plain
white jacket, and her hair was a lot looser, more like the
other girls'. She was descending into earth's atmosphere.

There was what you'd call a shocked silence. Not even
Mr. Nielson said anything for about a minute. He fussed
with the papers on his desk before looking up. "Splendid!
Simply splendid, Burke. I am pleased that you are not only
a fine musician, but a fine student of English literature.
Justine?''

I looked across the room and saw Justine's hand going
down. "Yes, Mr. Nielson, she is indeed splendid.'' That
was the windup. I tensed for the pitch. "I move you ask
Burke to give a report on this Andrew Marvell who is so
interesting. Yes, class?'' The Belle of the Bayou smiled
innocently, with revenge in those sparkling eyes.

"Yes!'' the class applauded.

Mr. Nielson looked a little uncertainly at Burke. "Do you agree, Burke?"

I saw her face as she turned to give Justine a quick glance. Inscrutable, as they say. But white—with the big animal eyes.

Her voice was as stiff as her back. "No. No, thank you. Some other time."

"Yes! Yes!" the class slyly insisted, clapping in rhythm. They were onto her. But I couldn't forget her eyes.

Mr. Nielson nodded. He's too trusting. "You are out-voted, I'm afraid, Burke. We will look forward to your oral report on Andrew Marvell, his life and works, a week from today. A ten-minute talk will be fine." He glanced at Burke, who sat sculpted in ice. Suddenly he got that daylight-is-dawning look as his eyes slid over the rest of us. Actually, he's not all that trusting. "As a matter of fact," he said with a thin smile, "it had already occurred to me that twice-weekly reports on great English literary figures would be a most profitable class project. I will ex-pect each of you to turn in the name of the author of your choice by tomorrow." He beamed on Burke. "Thank you, Burke, for leading off."

The guy behind me stage-whispered across the room at Justine, "Mouth!" He was right. She hadn't just axed Burke, she'd done a job on the rest of us.

Mr. Nielson left promptly when the noon buzzer sounded, and of course the class stampeded, all but Justine and me—and Burke. After a long couple of minutes of chilly silence, I picked up my books and the sack with the orchids and headed for the door. *"Two's* company," I said meaningfully to my subdued Miss Mouth, who hitched her book bag over a shoulder and followed. I brushed by Burke with a cool, "Excuse me."

I stepped outside, but the Snow Cone stuck out an arm, trapping Justine inside. "Just a minute," she said imperiously. "I want to talk to you, Justine."

"Not now, I thank you, Burke." Justine tried to push by the extended arm. "We have the noon show to do. Move, please."

"Not until you tell me *why* you did that to me! Don't you understand, Justine? I have never given an oral report before high-school students—my peers! This is only my *second* day in public school! Why did you attack me? What have I ever done to you? I had *thought* we could be friends!" The words poured out like suds at a beer bust. I was amazed. I was even more amazed when I caught a glisten in Burke's eyes. The Snow Cone—crying *again?*

I wasn't onto the plot yet, but I decided to ring down the curtain anyway. I grabbed the orchid stem out of the sack just as Justine yelled, "You move, you, Burke! Or I'll—I'll give you . . ."

"A punch in the nose" is what the Belle of the Bayou probably had in mind, but I stepped on her lines. "She'll give you these orchids, from both of us. Peace offering." I thrust the stem into Burke's hands. She looked surprised as her fingers closed around it. Catching Burke off guard, Justine pushed past. There was a loud ripping sound.

"Oh, my arm!" Burke stared at her jacket. "My sleeve—you've torn it!" A red spot was slowly spreading through the ragged rip. Justine and I looked question marks at each other, then our eyes locked onto the butterfly ring. I saw the sharp tips and got off on an instant guilt trip. I *knew* I should have finished burring and polishing that ring.

Burke's eyes swept over Justine. "You contemptible creature!" She dropped the orchids and ran.

"But I didn't . . ." Justine started to scream after her.

"It was an . . ." She stopped as Burke rounded a corner and disappeared. Suddenly she bent down, scooped up the orchid stem, and threw it in my face. One flower broke off. Mom's orchids!

I started to protest when she snatched off the ring, dropped it on the ground—and jumped on it! I was thunderstruck, as they say. My metals-class project!

"Hey now, wait just a . . ." I saw the ring, a sad, broken butterfly, flattened against the cement, and I leaned down to retrieve it. It was in two pieces—the butterfly, its wings badly twisted, and the band, which opened a little when I pushed at it. It was probably salvageable, with a little patience, and a lot of solder. I looked up, accusingly. "Now why'd you do . . . ?"

I was talking to the wind. She was gone. Things *can* always get worse. Murphy's Law.

★ ★ 4

While my hands did the dinner dishes that night, my head got busy plotting my new piece—The Cat Fight. No more impromptu pantomimes, I told myself sternly. Street interaction, yes. Stories, no. You can bet Marcel Marceau couldn't have pulled off his great "Bored Angel" act without a lot of practice—his hands had to learn how to be wing tips, moving gently in the heavenly winds; his body had to learn how to follow as he winged his way earthward. Would Maximilian Merriwether Murphy *ever* be up in lights at the Music Center?

I was the Murphy's built-in dishwasher. Mom was a saleslady at Bullock's, and on her feet all day; she figured she deserved a rest, once she got the dinner on. Dad hit the easy chair with the paper and TV: "Today in Sacramento," "Today at the White House," "Today on Wall Street." So here goes old slave labor into action at the sink. I wish I'd had a sister to take over. I didn't even have a brother. Only child, that's me, and I can tell you why people feel sorry for an only child.

Nobody mentioned the stem of orchids, stuck into my great-grandmother's thin crystal vase on the mantle, in the dimmest light in the house. I was figuring out how to casually bring up the subject when I heard Mom calling from the living room, where she was lying on the sofa reading *Time* magazine. I couldn't make out a word, so I stopped rinsing the dishes and shouted, "What's that, Mom? The water was running."

"I said, how was your day today, dear?"

I shouted, "Okay, Mom. A cat fight was all." The "cats" had turned tail. Justine was a no-show at noon, and Burke cut history.

"Don't shout, Max. I can hear you. I didn't know they allowed pets on campus. There are signs all over the place."

"You can't keep cats out of anywhere, Mom. And you can't stop a cat fight. It just has to run its course." I turned the water back on.

I heard a roar. I suspected it was Dad. Cringing slightly, I turned the water off. His voice came booming from the living room. "Max, why the devil'd you pick your mother's orchids?"

Mom was shushing and saying, "Now, Quentin . . ."

"I will not shh, Annie! Answer me, Max—and it better be good, unless you want a razor strop across the seat of your pants!" Dad had used an electric shaver for forever. *I* didn't even know what a razor strop looked like. And he had never lifted a finger against me since I was six years old, when the flat of his hand was enough to convince me that crime didn't pay. I had opened the gate and let the dog out, deliberately, and with malice aforethought. My theory was, then as now, that unfenced dogs had more fun. We didn't have a dog anymore. Vernon had died respectably of old age. But we had a character of a cat that liked to play in the water. Fat Cat—inspiration!

"Fat Cat, Dad!" I shouted.

Dad shouted, "Don't shout, Max—do you think I'm deaf? Fat Cat, eh? You expect me to believe that?"

Mom was shushing again. "Now, Quentin, I would have picked it anyway . . ."

"The boy's lying, Annie! *This* time I'm going to look up Granddad's old strop if it's the last . . ."

"I'm lying, Dad!" I shouted quickly. Confession was good for the soul, as they say, and with luck, good for the seat of the pants. Maybe there really *was* such a thing as a razor strop.

Suddenly Dad was standing in the doorway, glaring at me. I turned the tap on full, sending out strong ESPs to Fat Cat to get in here and play with the water. Where was he when I needed him to take the heat off me—with a cold stream in the face? My ESP was deteriorating.

"Dad, I got in bad with my girl. I thought the flowers would fix it up." The old red-ear act again. I knew Dad was watching.

"Did they?"

I splashed away with the dishes. "Yes—and no. In the long run, no. She threw them at me—and wrecked one."

"Learn anything?" There was a funny choking noise.

I turned to look at Dad. He was laughing out loud now. My mouth dropped open. "Well—yes. You could say so."

"You better say so," Dad said, gasping. "Because there won't be a next time, not with the orchids. I'm going to find that razor strop if it's the last thing I do. Finish the dishes and get on with your homework."

I did, and went to my room to look over an old book the school librarian had found buried in the stacks, and saved just for me: *Agna Enters On Mime*. It was a classic—with a heavy European slant, but I thought it might give me a deeper understanding of Marcel Marceau's work.

Personally, I preferred the light American touch—I guess I'd rather make people laugh than think. After all, it *was* pretty gut-wrenching to see Marceau's "Youth, Maturity, Old Age, and Death": fetal position and back to fetal position in sixty seconds.

I was so busy formulating my mime philosophy that I barely heard the phone ring. Mom knocked on my door. "It's for you, Max."

I went into the hall, which is a terrible place for a telephone—Grand Central Station, in our house. A sort of familiar man's voice came through the receiver. "This is Carter Lindstrom."

I said, "Uh, hello," like a little kid, a guilty little kid, but I couldn't think what I was guilty of.

"I'm glad you're the only Murphy on Ocean View Drive in the phone book. I'd like to know what happened to my daughter today—she seems quite ill. I had to bring her home from school early. She'll only say that something unpleasant happened. Nothing more. I'm hoping you can enlighten me, as you are the only one of her new friends whose name I know."

I smiled at the word *friend,* but I felt a real surge of admiration, as they say, for the Snow Cone. She had evidently not finked on Justine—or me, the innocent bystander. I thought fast.

"Well, sir," I said carefully, "she seemed worried about an assignment in English, an oral report." I hoped that would do it. It didn't.

"An oral report? I don't understand. Do you know how her sleeve came to be torn, and her arm scratched?"

I took a deep breath and dived in. "I think it was a little misunderstanding with another girl, sir—something to do with the oral report." Something, but not everything.

"Another student—attacked my daughter? She must be reported. Who is she?"

This was the moment of truth. I opted for it. "Sir, I know, but I can't say. It was strictly an accident." He didn't say anything. I fumbled on. "I'm not one to fink on my friends, sir."

"I won't ask you to 'fink' on your friends. Loyalty is sometimes an admirable quality, though frequently misplaced."

"I'm sorry if Burke got hurt, sir." But I wasn't worried. The brass butterfly wasn't all *that* lethal.

"She's very sensitive. She has to be, in her work. Yesterday it seems some young fool ridiculed her, although she made light of it. Today's incident, I'm afraid, casts still another shadow on your school. I'm disappointed, for my daughter's sake."

"Yes, sir," I gulped. She hadn't fingered me. Chalk up another plus for the Snow Cone.

"Yes. Well, good night, then, and thank you, Maximilian."

"Goodbye, sir." Why was it *my* school? Why was I feeling so responsible for this portable shadow Burke Lindstrom carried around with her? Mom was listening. "No, Mom, no trouble. None at all." Then, "I'm *not* lying, Dad. Yes, if I *am* lying about lying, you can take the razor strop to me. Any time, Dad."

It wasn't two minutes before the phone rang again. I had just gotten into Agna Enters' "Overture," but I rushed back into the hall, beating Mom.

"Hi, Justine. Uh, is that *you,* Justine? What's wrong with you?" There was a series of little gasps and groans. I shouted, "Why are you crying?"

"Don't shout at me, Maximilian, you! Do you think I'm

deaf, hahn?'' There was a great deal of repetition in my life.

"Well, *I'm* the one who should be crying," I said, warming to the subject. "What happened to the old show-must-go-on tradition, anyway? You left me in a bad spot at the High Noon gig."

"I cannot sing when I am crying, Maximilian! I have now started crying again! I do not *like* to be called—*contemptible creature*, me! That means—swamp rat and cottonmouth—and *skunk!* Oh, how I hate her! It was all (sob) *your* fault, Maximilian, yes?"

Another sensitive woman. That made two so far tonight. I started laughing. Right into the telephone. I couldn't quit. I was groaning with laughter. Occasionally I heard a gasp come through the earpiece. The sobs were gone. Finally I noticed my name being shouted over and over into my ear.

"Maximilian!" I stopped laughing. *"You* are a contemptible creature, you! An MCP—a male chauvinist hog—just like my Tante Celeste says!" There was a bang, not just a click.

Before I could slink into my room to lick my wounds, Dad shot me down. "Max, you're not wasting your time on that mime stuff tonight, are you? What are you doing there in your room? And it better be homework!"

"Well, uh, maybe a *little* mime work, Dad . . . But if I'm going to cut it as a professional . . ."

"You better cut it with UCLA, you hear me? You haven't even taken physics yet. You better get that in in your senior year or your name's mud, you hear me? And I want to see something better than a *C* in chemistry this term, you hear me, Max?"

"I hear you, Dad," I said, loudly enough to cover the guilt trip I was getting into.

"You *better* hear me, you hear me? UCLA only takes the top ten percent, and you better be in it! Forget this mime hogwash and get on with the show, you hear me?"

I heard him. Even though that last sentence made me smile, bitterly, his words quenched the fires of Agna Enters and Marcel Marceau in my soul. I had to make myself recall the great mission of mime, as Marceau described it: the breaking down and stylizing of component parts of reality.

Then I picked up reality as described by Quentin Murphy: Chem I. "Which should have a higher pH, a solution of primary sodium phosphate or primary amonium phosphate?"

Sometime soon I'd have to have the guts to tell Dad that pH is PU; that mime is magic; and that I was the Murphy who was going to repeal Murphy's Law.

★ ★ 5

For several days I hadn't exactly tried to stay away from
women. They had stayed away from me, until a phone call
too early Saturday morning, about seven o'clock. I didn't
hear the ring. Dad called crossly, "Max! Telephone!"

I sat up, dazed. There was a sharp rap on the door.
"Max—phone!" I struggled out of bed and into the hall.
"An emergency—*she* says. It better be good! Seven
o'clock on Saturday morning!" He took his hands off the
mouthpiece and handed me the phone.

"Maximilian, you've got to help me!" Burke's high-
pitched voice was practically hysterical. "I'm in such a
muddle—with Andrew Marvell! Oh, *please* come over and
help me!"

"Look, Burke," I said, letting my eyelids drift shut,
"it's too early, way too early, to cope with a coy mistress."

"What's that? An obscene phone call—from a *girl?*
Hang up on her, Max. Hang up!" Dad was standing at the
end of the hall, just outside his and Mom's room. I covered the mouthpiece with my hand and said discreetly, "It's
okay, Dad. It's a about a report for English."

The Snow Cone really sounded paranoid, talking faster
and louder by the second. I held the phone away from my

ear and projected, "Okay, okay. Stay cool." I did some fast figuring. I planned to resume my interrupted shut-eye until about ten. Then, Justine—or no Justine? "I'll be over at one. *Ciao*."

I dialed Justine. "Maximilian, you woke me up, you! What you are wanting?" She sounded annoyed, and I smiled smugly. I had forced her to break her vow of silence.

"Are we taking our bike ride this morning or not, Cherie? It would be kind of nice to know." Once again I stood back from the phone until she finished sputtering.

Finally I heard, "I am going shopping with Tante Celeste. All day, yes? Goodbye."

I sighed as I pulled the covers up under my chin. I'd miss my Louisiana lovely. But on the other hand, I had my closet door mirror. Time for mime.

At one o'clock I chained my bike to a light post in front of the Lindstrom condo. The place looked like your classic beach pad—lots of natural wood and red brick, with a forest of potted plants sprouting from the second and third floor balconies. The Lindstroms lived on the first floor; at the top of the steps, two potted palms flanked the front door. I pushed a lighted button, and heard a distant carillon playing inside. (The Murphy doorbell sounds like a Bronx cheer.)

Burke opened the door and we exchanged hi's, with me adding redundantly, "I'm here, Burke."

The corners of her mouth twitched. "Yes. Thank you for coming." She led me into the living room.

I could feel my eyes bugging out and my jaw coming unhinged. "Hey," I managed, looking around. "It's nice."

The whole room was white—and gold. The thick white rug was so deep you could sink into it and never be seen again. The white walls were splashed with white-framed paintings.

"Impressionist prints," Burke said. "Angelica adores Monet. And Manet and Pissarro and Renoir. She thinks my taste for Braque is quite gauche. But I love my print of *Musical Forms;* the original is in the Philadelphia Museum. Do you like Picasso's *Three Musicians?*"

"Well, er, sure. I think it's—great." Luckily I'd *heard* of Picasso.

"I detest it, although I *do* like *most* cubism."

"Matter of taste," I tossed off, quickly changing the subject. "Nice piano you've got there." It was the understatement of the year. The piano was all gold, one of those nine-foot-long jobs with heavily carved legs and a bench to match. It took up half the room. Mind-boggling.

"Do you like it? It's a Steinway, of course."

"Sure. I'd know a Steinway anywhere," I lied smoothly. "Well, let's get to work. I've got a job to go to at four. Shall we sit here?" I eyed the world's longest wraparound sofa—it looked like velvet, white velvet. I'd mentally staked out the section with the big matching ottoman.

"No. We'll use the study. Oh, Father." I turned and saw Mr. Lindstrom coming into the room. "You remember Maximilian Murphy."

I couldn't resist. "Probably not. I'm pretty *ordinary*— sir." As a matter of fact, it had been eating at me.

Mr. Lindstrom looked puzzled for a moment. Then he smiled and extended a hand. "You heard that? A snap judgment. I've lived to regret more than one of those, Maximilian. And I certainly apologize for that one." I hesitated for a moment, then we shook hands. "As a matter of fact, you're most extraordinary to give up a Saturday afternoon to help someone else with homework. Very generous of you, son."

Burke smiled and locked arms with her father. "Father's right, Maximilian. I do so hope to succeed at Mira Vista High School—he chose it very carefully for me for its high academic standing. And he should know—since he has been working in Belview Beach for the past five years."

"I thought you were new here," I said.

"We are—we moved here at the start of the semester. Until then, I was commuting from Hollywood—four freeways, twice a day!" Mr. Lindstrom laughed. "Fortunately, Burke's mother doesn't have far to go to *her* work—just one freeway does it now."

Burke frowned at the word "mother" I noticed, and turned quickly to her father. "Father is with the Belview Beach Branch of Southern California Bank."

"Right," I said. "SCB is where I have *my* account." Of course I didn't declare my assets. For under five-hundred dollars I preferred to be a man of mystery.

"Father's a vice president." She said it so proudly you'd have thought she meant vice president of the U.S., at least.

"Well, you two help yourselves to the study. I'm glad Burke is getting some help with that report, Maximilian. It's tearing her apart. By the way, if you have time to look over the Auburn, it's in the garage."

I grinned. "Thanks—sir."

The study was a giant book nook. Books lined all the walls, clear up to the ceiling. The rug, the heavy library table, the leather game-room chairs, the free-standing Swedish stove in one corner, and the love seat facing it were—no guesswork needed—white. In our family, we give dirt-color high priority. Even the background of our prize old Chinle Navajo rug, inherited from my grandfather, is good, practical dirt-color.

Burke spread out her papers and books on the table, and we sat down next to each other. "I'm glad you know my father a little better now," she said. "You may possibly get to meet my mother later. She's working today. I'm afraid she's a workaholic."

"Where does she work? My mom's working today, too—at Bullock's."

"Oh, yes? Angelica has her own ad agency, in Westwood. L'Agence Angelica Lindstrom." Of course, doesn't everybody's mom? When I didn't say anything, she went on. "It's a small agency, but she handles some very big accounts."

"Like which?" I expected American Motors (with its classy Alliance), or Princess Cruises (to up-scale Acapulco), or Texaco (whose Star car won the Indy 500).

What I got was, "Like Van Alston."

"Van Alston?"

"Raoul Van Alston. He had just one wire and cable service plant when my mother took on his account. Now he has seven in four states, distributing nationwide, and all because of Angelica's slogan, 'Van Alston: the Wizard of Wire.' It may sound simple, but it takes talent to create a slogan that sells."

It sounded stupid. I shrugged noncommittally. "Let's begin on old Andy or we'll never end."

She picked up a sheet of paper. "I wonder if I should delete the references to Donne and Ben Jonson."

"Judging from that stack of papers, if you don't delete

something, your report's going to run way over ten minutes.'' I wish that was *my* problem. I was always looking for padding.

"Well, I won't let William Blake go. He was slightly paranoid, but terribly interesting.'' She pulled out the Blake notes.

"Let him go, Burke. Blake the Flake wasn't even in the same century.'' I took the sheet from her and folded it up. "Save him. You can use him in another report. And you can bet there'll be another . . . and another . . .''

"Mr. Nielson's assigning a lot of work, but I think he wants to be fair.'' I had to agree with that—too fair. "It's just that I'm not used to deadlines of this sort. When I had a tutor, I was free to fit my assignments into any schedule that didn't interfere with my practicing and performances. Music always comes first.''

I looked at her. "Why didn't you *tell* Mr. Nielson, if it's too hard for you to have this ready by Tuesday? He's a pretty nice guy.''

"No, I'm trying not to make waves. I want to fit into a normal school pattern. Maximilian, I want to avoid . . . being different.''

"Well, *viva la difference,*'' I said grandly, blowing my French accent. "Most M.V. girls would *kill* to be different like you—you know, white cashmere sweaters, gold chains—*that* different.'' Impulsively, I reached across the table to touch her hand. My hand never made it. She snatched hers away with a horrified gasp that left me feeling like the village rapist. "Hey,'' I said, wounded. "Nothing personal, needless to say.''

"Oh, *don't,* Maximilian!'' Don't what? Don't touch me, you leper—don't apologize—don't put me down? The wild look left her eyes as suddenly as it had come, and she bent over the work on the table. "I mean—my *mother* chooses all my clothes. She has beautiful taste, but we have had to learn how high school girls dress." Silence.

I filled in the dead air, nervously prattling advice that nobody asked for—a pitfall Dad had warned me about. "I think you should have stayed with your tutor. You sure know more English Lit. than the rest of us. Anyway, I can't see why anybody would pick Mira Vista."

"I *could* have gone to Beverly Hills High School. That was my mother's choice. But that's a wealthy school with strong show business connections, and what I was looking for was a cross section of students in a school with good academics."

"Well, nice try. What do you think of old M. V. now?"

She picked up a ballpoint pen—white—and held it poised in the air while she thought. "I'm not ready to say. It has just been a week. However, I believe it is the *real world,* whether I like it or not."

"The real world? Not in my book! The *real world's* out there—where you make it professionally, the way *you're* doing with your fiddle. Mira Vista's a crock!"

Her eyes were sizing me up—or down. "And you plan to make it professionally, as a mime, Maximilian?"

"Sure. I'm on my way. I don't plan to spend any more time in a two-bit high school than the law requires." I didn't tell her I'd just found out from the Admissions Office that the law required me to either stay in school full-time until I'm eighteen or else to graduate with a diploma, and that even with an official "State of California High School Certificate of Proficiency" I'd have to con my parents into signing a release for me to drop out any sooner. This loomed as an annoying—but not impossible—hurdle.

"What is your background in mime?" She was trying

to confuse me, or maybe she wasn't trying, but she managed to do it anyway.

"Background? Well, there's the High Noon Show every day. There's the performance five days a week, and the practice at home for it—except for audience interactions." I had suddenly remembered, and she picked right up on it.

"That wasn't an interaction, Maximilian. That was character assassination." She smiled. "Go on. What else?"

"I like to work with kids, so one Sunday afternoon a month I'm a recreation department volunteer. About six of us go to the Inner-City Playhouse in Los Angeles to put on a show for poor kids, then help them put on their own. They really dig mime, especially."

"That's a coincidence, Maximilian. The Van Alstons have just endowed a wing for the Damaged Children's Foundation—that's a boarding school for autistic and abused children. Ann-Oliveras says she's looking for a mime to work with them. It's a new kind of therapy."

"Hey, that *is* a coincidence!" She had gotten my attention. "I'll be available after June."

"Really? I'll mention your name to her. The job is just right for a student. It's part time and minimum pay, Ann says, but should be marvelously rewarding, emotionally, and very fulfilling."

I said quickly, "Well, thanks—but don't mention my name yet. I have some commitments at the Village Mall— that is, there's been a lot of interest—er, *some* interest, by La Belle Cuisine—that pots and pans place; The Chocolate Box, and Little Nothings—that's ladies lingerie . . ."

She glanced at me shrewdly. "What exactly have you *done?* Have you studied with a professional mime? Have you taken classes in theater arts? Have you played in any of the little theaters?"

Why was I sacrificing my Saturday to this turkey, anyway? She had *me* on the chopping block! "Hey, now, wait a minute, Burke. Maybe I'm no genius like you're supposed to be, but . . ."

"Maybe you *are,* but you're not very *smart,* Maximilian." My mouth dropped open. Just who was helping whom, as they say, here today? "What I mean is, if mime is what you want, you've got to go for it. The arts aren't the easy way to earn a living. Whatever made you want to be a mime, in the first place?"

"Let's get on with our work," I snapped. Why should I tell *her* about that great mime, Kenny Power Wilson, at the Sand Hill Fair two years ago? I had followed him around all afternoon, squeezing through the crowds thronging the food and game booths.

"Well, yes, we really must. And after all, it is *your* problem, Maximilian. I'm going to have to memorize all this tomorrow—that means finishing it today, and I still have three more hours of practicing."

"Burke, *don't* memorize it. Talk from notes."

"I'm going to memorize it. I've decided on that. I can't take a chance on inaccurate wording. The class would laugh. I'm used to memorizing, Maximilian. I even memorize all my work for our informal 'Evenings with Burke Lindstrom.' You've never heard of them, of course." It wasn't even a question.

Annoyed at being labeled a cultural illiterate, I didn't reply. The "Evenings" were, she explained, as though to a child, dress rehearsals at the Lindstrom home for her concerts, and were "celebrated in musical circles."

I'd had enough of the Snow Cone. I said shortly, "Meanwhile back at the ranch, as they say . . ."

We put in a solid hour's work before Mr. Lindstrom

called from somewhere in the house, "Pizza man's here, Princess. You and Maximilian clear off a place at your table."

My mouth started watering. I hoped the pizza was deep-dish Chicago style.

"Have you checked it carefully, Father?"

"All's well," he called back.

"Why's he checking it out?" A pizza's a pizza, unless you're looking for mozzarella and mushrooms and what you get is anchovies and olives.

"Cockroaches." She said it matter-of-factly.

"Roaches? How come?" It was the answer I had least expected.

"You can't be too careful, Maximilian, about cock-roaches. They're simply *swarming* in those commercial kitchens, you know. Why, I found one, drowned in my cup of hot chocolate at the Singing Geese, that expensive little bistro on Sunset Boulevard in Beverly Hills."

My eyes were doing a mime routine, wide and rolling. Finally I managed to say, "Personally, I've never seen a cockroach in a restaurant. But we never go anywhere but the Steak Space, anyway. In my family, cheap is gour-met."

"We go there, too, Father and I." Burke Lindstrom—the *Music Center* Burke Lindstrom—at the Steak Space? Of course the steaks are good and the service fast, but it's pretty declassé, as they say. "I like it because you can watch the cooking."

"I couldn't care less about watching it," I said. "It's eating it that's my bag."

Burke's dad came in carrying a tray loaded with the pizza, tall glasses of what turned out to be canned iced tea, and plates and real napkins.

"Enjoy." He smiled at us and left.

I helped myself to half the pizza. It hung over the plate so I double-decked it. "Hey, he's okay," I said before I stuffed my mouth.

"He's my best friend." She was looking proud again. "He was also my manager, until this year. I'm with International Artists now. But it's my *father* who deserves the credit for whatever success I've had." She took just one little wedge of the pizza. I had my eye on the rest of it.

"You mean *you* had nothing to do with your success?" I smiled, and she smiled back. You could almost call her pretty, when she smiled.

"I did the practicing."

"Where do you keep your fiddle?" I glanced around the room.

"In my bedroom. Would you like to see my Guadagnini?" She got up from the table. "I'll get it. I'm *very* proud of it."

She was back in seconds with a violin made of dark wood polished to a soft sheen. I noticed she held it by the neck with a napkin covering her hand. She saw me staring at the napkin. "All fingers are oily," she said. "Father almost got into trouble in London because he wouldn't let the customs people handle it."

"I thought fiddles were a sort of beige, like guitars. Are you planning to finish off the pizza?"

"No, help yourself." I did. "This color is called plum, and it's very special. Father got it at auction—the Sotheby Parke Bernet people."

"I'll bet it cost a bundle," I probed impolitely.

She said casually, "It cost eighty thousand, and it's worth more today." I stared, unbelieving. A fiddle—worth eighty thou? "Now we're shopping, Father and I, for a

Guarnerius. That may run over two hundred thousand.'' I almost choked on my last bite of pizza. That seemed like all the money in the world—for one little wooden fiddle? And it wasn't even a Strad. I'd heard of that, at least. ''In my opinion, it's a finer instrument than a Stradivarius,'' she added, reading my mind. She took the plum-colored Fort Knox back to her bedroom, and I got my act together.

I didn't like the awe that was sweeping over me. She was just an M.V. junior who needed help with an assignment, I kept telling myself. When she came back we got down to cases and worked until my deadline, three-fifteen.

''Courage, Camille,'' I said at the door as I was leaving. ''Remember you're not exactly giving a speech to the United Nations. What you're doing is holding an easy little Morning with Burke Lindstrom for a few friends. Okay?''

It was too late to see the Auburn. The front door had just closed after Burke's, ''Thank you, Maximilian,'' when I heard a surprised ''Oh!'' coming from the Strand in front of the condo. I turned and saw a woman reeling back from the light post where I'd chained my bike. And speeding down the Strand in a zebra-striped bikini was no doubt the cause of it all, Hit-and-Run Teitelbaum.

I rushed over to the woman. ''Are you all right, ma'am?'' I took hold of her, steadying her.

She looked at me in surprise. I returned the look—for a different reason. She was one of those sultry green-eyed ''You've-come-a-long-way-Baby'' magazine blurbs come to life—a slim bottle-blonde wearing white dollar signs.

''Why—thank you. Yes—I'm all right. Skaters are a frightful hazard, aren't they? The girl probably didn't see me coming around the corner of the house, though.'' Her hand went to her left eye. I glanced at it.

"I'm afraid you're going to have a shiner, ma'am—miss. Can I help you to your house?"

Just as I said that, the Lindstroms' front door banged open and Burke and her father came barreling out, shouting, "Angelica!" They brushed me aside and surrounded her, but she waved them away. Mr. Lindstrom tried to put an arm around her.

"Oh, stop it, Carter. I'm perfectly able to walk. That skater"—we all squinted down the Strand, but Trinka had become nothing but a dot in the distance—"didn't see me and I jumped out of her way, right into the light post and this wretched bike." I cringed. There was a big grease spot on her white skirt. So this was Burke's mom. Angelica. I couldn't help smiling, noticing her white accordion-pleated sleeves that moved like wings.

She turned and saw me and frowned. "Thank you, young man." It was a definite dismissal.

"This is Maximilian Murphy, my friend from school, Angelica," Burke put in. Mrs. Lindstrom didn't even glance my way.

I said, "Better put a beefsteak on that eye, ma'am."

"Ours are frozen, Maximilian," Burke said.

That was two down. I didn't want to strike out, so I said, "See you," to her and got busy unlocking my bike, the "wretched" one. I'd bet the lady's green cat-eyes weren't exactly beaming on me, as Burke and her dad eased her towards the condo.

Just before I swung onto the banana seat of my Strand cruiser, planning to head for the nearest exit to the bike path, I heard what Mom calls, reprovingly, a "shouting match." The noise was coming from the Lindstroms', so naturally I tuned in, while I pretended to straighten a few spokes on my front wheel.

". . . neglecting your practicing for some stupid high-school boy, Burke!" The winged woman. I bent low over my wheel. ". . . with the Houston concert coming up, and before that our first Evening here at the beach! Just how do you . . ." The voice faded and the words blurred.

". . . I'm not yelling any louder than you are, Angelica!" Burke, yelling. "Have I ever failed you, tell me that, have I?"

"Once! And you remember that, Burke, you remember what happened!" There was a low-pitched cry, like a hurt animal. I wished I could get my feet moving. ". . . Miss High and Mighty! And it better not be when the Van Alstons are here! And *Abe* is coming . . ."

Then a firm command. "Quiet! The *boy* is still out there." Mr. Lindstrom.

I left. Another cat fight. How come they were all around me since Burke Lindstrom came to town?

★ ★ 6

I found the original in a 1951 *Esquire* magazine that I'd luckily picked up at a garage sale. There it was: the Sensational, Sexy MG-TD! The foxiest female I'd ever seen was curled up on the red hood. I'd give a month's pay to meet that blonde in the gold fringe—then I counted back, and realized she was by now old enough to be my grandmother. This brought me up short with time and mortality.

"There isn't enough time, Rabbit," I puffed, as we ran up one of Belview Beach's too-steep hills—paved-over dunes—at six-thirty Tuesday morning.

"For what, Mox?" he said easily. I wished there was a drop of Tarahumara in my blood. He'd told me how his Grandfather Rabbit and the old Rabbit's buddies had often raced up and down the mountains surrounding Copper Canyon in Mexico, kicking a ball ahead of them, for three days and nights.

"For everything I want to do. The Kola King Marathon! The Olympics, someday! My car! Mime—my career! Women!"

"You don' need time for women, Mox. Stay away from them like I do or you won' have time for anythin' else."

"So Latins are lousy lovers!" I hooted. "Anyway the

Proficiency Test is at the top of my list right now. You remember I told you I'm checking out of school this June with a Certificate instead of going a whole year longer for a diploma!'' I was shouting—and puffing.

The Rabbit turned to look at me and slowed his pace. "I thought maybe you change' your mine, Mox. How're we goin' to train together? Your papa will be one mad papa, I think, Mox! He don' want you to be no dummy!''

"I'm no dummy right now, Rabbit! I'm getting my act together, as they say, and I'm taking it on the road in June—over at the shopping mall!'' I raced up to him. *"We'll* train together! We'll figure it out when the time comes!''

The Rabbit glanced at his drugstore digital watch—a Christmas bonus from Paco, his boss. The Rabbit worked from five to nine P.M. weekdays and twelve-hour weekends at Paco's Tacos, an eight-stool Mexican eat-in/take-out shack that served the best soft tacos in town. Paco only hired illegals. He paid them below minimum, and they worked their tails off for him. Only Paco and the Rabbit could speak English, so when you called in to order, some Mexican on the other end would shout, *"Bueno!"* then drop the receiver, letting it dangle against the wall until Paco or the Rabbit could get to it. The Rabbit was valuable, so Paco paid him twenty-five cents an hour more than the other guys.

"Mox—that las' mile—seven-two! That's bad! Now le's pour it on!'' He leaped away from me like a frog's leg in a frying pan, as Justine puts it.

Fifteen minutes before the lunch buzzer sounded, Mr. Nielson asked Burke to come to the rostrum. She didn't have any notes to hold, and for a second or two she didn't seem to know what to do with her hands as she turned and faced the class. Then she gripped the rostrum on both sides as if it were trying to escape. I sat in the back of the room, bent over the pages of the speech she had given me.

"I have memorized concertos and long recital pieces," she had said, somberly. "But, Maximilian, this is different."

She looked good in that man-tailored white silk shirt stuffed into her white jeans. She wore a white and gold-striped scarf knotted at her throat, and on one arm a wide gold bracelet that had the soft sheen of the real stuff. She *still* wasn't one of your average M.V. girls, Mom Lindstrom.

"This talk is on Andrew Marvell, an English poet and pamphleteer of the Puritan Period, that is to say, the years between 1640 and 1660, during the Long Parliament when Oliver Cromwell was Lord Protector of England . . ."

"I thought the Puritan Period was in 1620, when the Pilgrims landed at Plymouth Rock . . ."

Mr. Nielson tapped his pencil loudly on the student desk where he was sitting with the class. "Stacey, you will please not interrupt. It is not only rude, but disruptive for the speaker. Please go on, Burke."

Burke looked a little shaken, holding onto the rostrum tighter than ever. I couldn't see her knees, but five'll get you ten they were buckling.

"Yes." Her voice was as firm and cold as Mom's cheesecake, which she always freezes before serving. I looked up to see if Burke needed prompting. She didn't. "Marvell was born in 1621, the son of a Church of England parson. Young Marvell was educated at Cambridge, graduating in 1638. He was at first a Royalist . . ."

"You mean he was king? What—hic—happened to Cromwell?"

"Stacey, you have just earned a failing grade for the entire week. Please leave the classroom." Mr. Nielson shook his pencil towards the door. "I'm going to call your parents."

There was a pause while Spacey Stacey left the room, giggling and swaying a little. I felt sorry for Burke. She stared, deadpan, straight at the class. When she started to talk again, her voice was like a robot's. Little beads of sweat stood out on her forehead, but it wasn't all that hot in the room.

"He later became a confirmed Republican and supporter of the Commonwealth. During his lifetime he was famous for his political and ecclesiastical pamphlets. While he was a member of Parliament, he published a newsletter to his constituents . . ."

"Mr. Nielson, I'm sorry, sir, but may I have permission to go to the can?" A ripple of sniggers was followed by a rolling wave of laughter.

Mr. Nielson stood up. "Stop it *now,* class!" There was a sudden silence. "If absolutely necessary, Mark. Proceed, please, Burke."

She waited until Mark left the room. He's a churl and everyone knew why he left and why he wouldn't be coming back. I think she knew too, but she went grinding doggedly along, some wild, thin strands of hair sticking to her face, glued on with sweat. I don't know why, the Snow Cone was nothing to me, but I really wanted her to make it with this dumb report. I guess I admire a fighter. I found my place in the speech, and got so busy pulling for her I didn't notice she had stopped talking. I glanced up, surprised, and saw her staring at me, her violet eyes taking up her whole face.

She was supposed to be getting into Marvell's poetry. I decided a hint was better than a holler, so I discreetly mimed an imaginary girl in my arms, and she picked up on it. Burke's a weirdo, but she's not a stupid weirdo.

"Yes. Marvell's poetry wasn't really appreciated during his lifetime . . ." Her voice was shaking now, and I went into my best ESP: Come on, Burke, you can do it! *"To His Coy Mistress* was written circa 1650 . . ."

"What's 'circa'?" This time it was Marvin Gross, the Mean and the Gross.

Mr. Nielson never tumbled. "About. About 1650. Go on, Burke."

"It has overtones of the Cavalier poets in it—although Marvell is more aligned with the Lyricists. For instance, Robert Herrick's poem 'Gather ye rosebuds while ye may,/ Old Time is still a-flying,/ And this same flower that smiles today,/ Tomorrow will be dying,' certainly has overtones of Marvell's 'Had we but world enough and time,/ This coyness, lady, were no crime.' In other words, *carpe diem.*"

"Crappy dame." It was just a mutter, but everyone in the room could hear it. Mr. Nielson was on his feet again, and I have never seen him so mad.

"Who said that?"

It was Mean Marvin the Gross, of course, who else? But nobody would fink. *"Who said that?"* Mr. Nielson thundered, and we all shrank down in our seats.

"Excuse me." Our heads turned from Mr. Nielson to Burke. She ran out the open door, looking sick. I started to get up—she needed help.

"Just a minute, Maximilian!" Mr. Nielson roared. I froze on my feet, at my desk. "You are *all* to hear this! For your thoroughly rotten treatment of a fellow student, you are *all*—I said *all*—hereby assigned a five-page *written* report on the Pearl Poet's *Sir Gawain and the Green Knight!* As translated in prose form beginning on page one ninety-four of your textbook. A week from today! *No exceptions!* Class dismissed!"

Urp! I *hated* that medieval stuff. Sir Gawain! Thanks, Burke, thanks a lot. Then I remembered it wasn't *her* fault, and she was probably being sick, sicker, sickest—maybe dead, somewhere on campus. Maybe she was in a restroom . . . I turned and grabbed Justine's hand.

"Come on, Cherie. We've got to help her. She might be pretty sick somewhere." I pulled her along with me across the campus.

"But, Maximilian, I am not speaking to you! Did you forget?" She was breathless.

"Of course I forgot! That's what love is all about, Cherie—you are *supposed* to forget the bad parts!" I squeezed her hand.

"Yes, Maximilian?"

"Of course! Where do you think she'd be—where would you be, if you got sick like Burke probably is?"

"Stop, Maximilian!" She pulled me to a stop. "I cannot think when I am running." She caught her breath. "I would *not* be at the pavilion."

"Go on!" I put my arm around her waist and squeezed it.

"And I would not be at the cafeteria, or where too many people could see me." She considered, for a moment. "I would be sitting all by myself behind a building. Or I would be very sick in the restroom." She paused. "Yes, that is it."

"Let's check behind the buildings, first." We started off at a trot. We checked home ec, the science building, the social sciences. Then we came to the shop buildings. We found her lying on a bench behind metals shop, the same bench I usually head for during my metals-class break. Her face was the same color as the building—off-white. Her eyes were closed. She was so still she looked dead. Justine rushed up to her and grabbed her by the shoulders.

"Burke, Burke! Are you dead, you? Speak to me!"

"Oh, Justine!" She started to cry. At least she wasn't dead. I stepped up and started to help her sit up. She jerked away from me. "Don't—touch me!" She seemed to focus on me for the first time. "Oh, it's *you*, Maximilian."

"Let her alone, Maximilian! *I* will take care of her!" Justine put her arms around Burke, and drew the red head down on her shoulder. "There, Burke, you are fine," she said soothingly, probably just the way she talked to one of her little brothers back on the bayou.

"Well, you don't look fine," I said loudly, annoyed at being treated like Typhoid Mary for the third time. "You look sick!"

"Maximilian, you are thinking that helps Burke?" Justine looked at me accusingly.

Burke sat up straight. "I'm not half as sick as I was. I threw up in the restroom." I was glad we had opted for the search behind the buildings first.

"Be careful now, Burke. Don't move too fast," Nurse Landry said, putting an arm around Burke's shoulders.

"Oh, Justine—Maximilian! why did they treat me that

way? It was a *good* report!'' She swiped at her eyes, and squared her shoulders.

"They didn't *all* hassle you, Burke,'' I said. "Only a couple or three flakes. Don't let it get to you.'' It already had, of course.

"Do you want to go home, Burke?'' Justine asked.

"I can call your father for you. At the bank,'' I offered.

"No—thank you. He's out to lunch anyway. Please tell me the truth—wasn't it a good report?''

"It was an *A*-plus, wait and see. The jerks were jealous is all.'' How could I really tell her the truth? She'd switched from that frumpy dress to jeans and shirts, and she was *still* different. It wasn't all to do with clothes. Burke Lindstrom didn't know how to be ordinary.

Burke stood up, Justine beside her. "You two are just— wonderful friends.'' She hugged Justine. "Thank you, Justine. And Maximilian.'' She smiled at me, wanly. I didn't hug her. I learn pretty fast.

"Burke, you need more *fun,*'' Nurse Landry counseled. *"I* think you work too hard. You are to come bike riding with Maximilian and me. On Saturday. Yes, Maximilian?''

I was speechless, which seldom happens. My Cherie, inviting another woman along on a Saturday? "Hey now,'' I blustered, "that's a great idea! Come on, Burke, say yes.'' I was hoping she'd say no. She didn't.

"Oh, I love biking! Father and I ride, occasionally! Where will we go?'' A little color was coming into her face.

"To Venice. Little Sodom by the Sea,'' I said.

Justine laughed. "So don't forget, Burke. What are you going to do now?'' she added anxiously.

Burke said, "I'm going to the nurse's office to lie down

for a while. Then I'll call Father to come pick me up. Thank you, both of you.'' She bestowed a radiant smile on us, and turned and walked away on somewhat wobbly legs.

"Be careful, *chère!*'' Justine called.

I swept my cute Cajun into my arms. "I love you, Florence Nightingale.''

She started to say, "No feelies . . .'' but I cut her off with a kiss.

"Of course not. Me—feelies? I am merely a student of languages. What's that message on your T—'*CODOFIL— Non!*' '' I held her off at arm's length, studying the, er, message.

She said with sudden verve, "It means Council on the Development of French in Louisiana. It means French French—*non, cher!* It means Cajun French—but yes!''

"Hmmm. I never thought I'd love an activist. Close your eyes when you kiss, Jane Fonda.''

★ ★ 7

The three of us sat on the patio of the Seagull Cafe, next to the low brick wall that separated it from Venice's Ocean Front Walk. We were all wearing shorts and T's. The weather had gone berserk and dished up a Southern Hemisphere summer in the midst of a Northern Hemisphere winter. It was another day of "a high of seventy-six at the beaches, eighty-six in the Valley," thanks to the Santa Ana winds that swept in, hot and dry from the desert, under a layer of marine air. An inversion, we called it. Every weekend during the winter, the Under Thirties do an inversion dance. (Dad hated Santa Anas. They meant high water bills. He was doing his rain dance.)

"It is nice!" Justine said, looking around the patio. There were fresh flowers on every table. "It is just like New Orleans—you know the Vieux Carré?"

Burke said promptly, "I've never been to New Orleans, but sidewalk cafes remind me of Paris."

"Ah so," I said. "It reminds *me* of the Doughnut Hole in downtown L.A. You sit out on the sidewalk at barrel tables and dunk your doughnuts, you snobs." I grinned at them.

"So what'll it be, guy and gals?" The waiter had finally

made it to our table. His mustache twitched when he smiled.

"I would like the Ravishing Omelet," Justine said, and I could swear the waiter gave her a wink, but maybe he just had sand in his eye.

"Everything on it? Spinach, leeks, mushrooms, walnuts, tomatoes, powdered deer's horn?"

"Hold the deer's horn," I said straight-faced. "She doesn't need it."

"Is it healthful?" Justine demanded.

"Yeah, baby, but you don't need it, the man says. And what's for you, Miss?" The waiter turned to Burke.

She was studying the menu with a frown. "I'd like a cheese omelet, please. And if you don't mind, I'd like to watch your cook prepare it."

Justine's eyebrows shot up, but it was no surprise to me.

The waiter kept his cool. Kooks, druggies, and exhibitionists were a dime a dozen, as they say, on Ocean Front Walk. "Why not, your ladyship?"

Burke stood up, adding, "And herb tea, please."

I opted for the house's Belcher Burger with the Green Giant Omelet on the side. "And rush it, you see a starving artist sitting here."

Over on a green patch bordering the walk, a barbershop quartet was trying out some of the oldies from the fifties and sixties, "Rock Around the Clock," "Little Bitty Pretty One," "Blue Suede Shoes." A black giant, looming two feet over the populace, was doing a Harlem Globetrotter dazzler—twirling a basketball on the tip of one finger held high over his head. Skaters were everywhere, disco-ing to high-decibel portable radios.

"You are going to put on a show today, like always,

Maximilian?'' Justine beamed on me. I loved my resident
claque.

"You bet. But I'm going to eat first. I may be sluggish
working on a full stomach, but I'd be dead on an empty
one.''

The waiter eventually came back, balancing a big tray.
Burke was following him.

"It was all right, so far as I could see,'' she said.

"Would you care to do an endorsement for the Seagull,
Miss?'' the waiter said, pulling out the chair for her after
he had set down the tray on a stand. "No droppings in the
Danish, no feathers on the fish, no cockroaches in the cock-
a-leekie?''

After eating half the burger and all the omelet, I decided
I'd better get on with the show while I could still step over
the little wall.

"Under pain of death,'' I told my women, "don't let
anyone touch my plate. Now don't take your eyes off me!
And clap, clap, clap! It's okay to throw money!''

Just as I got halfway over the wall, the waiter appeared
out of nowhere and caught me by the shirttail. "Skipping
out on the bill, Mac?''

"Now cut that out!'' I yelled. "Can't you see I'm leaving my women as security? And don't you lay a finger on
my plate! I'm only half through!''

"I've got all the women I can handle, Mac. What's your
game, anyway?'' He didn't let go of my shirt.

"Mime, you dolt, mime! Let go of me, and I'll prove
it! Anyway, not to worry. The beautiful redhead can foot
the bill if I dematerialize.''

"Just step back over here, Mac, while I ask her.'' It
was a bad scene. I saw Burke laugh as she pulled a bill
from the pocket of her tailored white shorts. The creep of

a waiter nodded towards me. "You can go over the wall now, Mac. Break a leg!"

I stepped over the wall with dignity. Then I took my mime mask from a back pocket of my cut-off jeans, and white cotton gloves from a side pocket. Next I walked a small circle, clearing the people from it with an authoritarian sweep of my hands. Now I was ready.

A fair-sized audience had already gathered. Some of the skaters were standing on their toe stops, watching, and a bongo group had stopped drumming to come over and stare. The lunch bunch at the Seagull was in my pocket, and miscellaneous strollers stopped at the circle: a couple of Indians from India, the lady in a bright sari; a scattering of skinheads in saffron robes, shabby jogging shoes sticking out beneath ragged hems; a couple of bag ladies, stopping by with their "borrowed" shopping carts labeled "Ralph's" and "Safeway."

I made a low, elaborate bow, stretching my arms wide. There was a sprinkling of applause, but this was a wait-and-see audience. I decided to start with my new bicycle act, beginning the gig in "neutral;" facing the audience, feet just slightly apart and pointing out, arms relaxed. I stood near the red brick wall, turning my right side to the biggest crowd—those outside the wall.

Standing on my left foot, I "pedaled" vigorously with my right, leaning into the invisible handlebars. As I "rode" along, I smiled and tipped my hat and waved to imaginary pedestrians, and once "braked" sharply when an invisible dog ran in front of me. It wasn't easy; every time my right foot went down towards the ground, my left knee had to do a deep bend, in sync.

There was a burst of applause, and I acknowledged it by tipping my imaginary hat, then "parking" my bike. I mimed getting off the seat, and went to shake hands with a kid, a girl about twelve years old, in the inner circle. I had picked her carefully. She was laughing hard, and had bright, intelligent eyes. In mime, I bowed and smiled and invited her, with a sweep of my hand, to ride tandem with me. She shook her head, suddenly shy, but I held out my hand insistently. She finally took it and I "helped" her climb onto the bike, a spot on the pavement just behind me.

I gagged it up a lot, trying to "hold" the imaginary bike with her on the rear seat. When I missed my footing and "fell," the audience roared with laughter. I've found that watching someone else make a fool of himself is pure fun— it cuts close to the gut but never leaves a mark! I finally managed to "climb" on, and with much turning around to reassure my co-rider, much silent laughter at her trepidations, and with elaborate hand signals, I finally "sped" off. I was right about the little girl. She was a quick study. When we finally "crashed" the bike, she fell off with me like an old pro. The applause and the laughs were deafening, as they say.

I gave my coartist a gift. It isn't easy to blow up one of those long, thin balloons clowns always carry. The trick is in a mighty first *huff*, accompanied by a quick stretching of the rubber with the hands. I had finally acquired the technique after nearly losing my hearing from balloons bursting in my ears! I knotted the balloon and twisted it, and it became a cute, blue beagle. The girl laughed, and shook my hand.

I got so carried away with my great success that I did three more interaction gigs. The last one was with the giant with the basketball. The ball we "played" with, though, was imaginary. Naturally he "beat" me fair and square.

The guy turned out to be Mile-High Mulligan of the Lakers. It was my turn to be impressed.

He grinned, "Where's my balloon, mime?"

I said, "Sure thing. I didn't know you'd want one, Mile-High." He had about everything money could buy—a mansion, a movie-star wife, a half-dozen cars.

"For my little girl," he said, winking broadly.

"Right." I blew up a long red balloon, and created a dachshund, the shortie of the dog world. "Meet Mile-Low," I said.

When I finally remembered my women and my Belcher Burger, I shot back over the brick wall, full of love and good fellowship for the whole world. Burke was missing.

"You were very funny, Maximilian. I didn't let them take your plate, *cher*," Justine said. She saw me staring at Burke's empty chair. "She left, her. Just a few minutes ago, Maximilian. She said she had to go home."

"Hey, we can't let her take off alone. Her Dad told us to take good care of her, remember? She's a sheep among wolves. Where's the bill?"

"She paid it. You stayed away just long enough, Maximilian!" She smiled and took my hand.

"Well, Cherie, I didn't plan it that way! Come on, we'll catch her at the bikes. They're all chained up together." I pushed through the people, pulling Justine behind me.

"But I went with her, *cher,* and we unlocked the chain and she took her bike."

"Oh, no! Why'd you do that?" We got to the bikes. And there were our two. The white one was missing.

"Burke said you might be hours longer, you were having such a good time, you."

"Holy Sacramento, isn't that her about half a block up

the bike path? It's sure a redhead in a white outfit! And she's going the wrong way, north instead of south!'' I unlocked our bikes, and we climbed on. ''There's some dude riding beside her! Come on, let's pour it on!''

''Maybe he is stealing her,'' Justine said helpfully.

We tore down the bike trail as fast as we could, considering the wacko skaters waltzing backwards and forwards right over the big letters on the paving, BIKES ONLY. There were also the Saturday strollers with their dogs and toddlers. It was a maze. Of course Burke and her ''captor'' couldn't go any faster either, so we could still track them less than a block ahead.

The Santa Monica Pier soon appeared, jutting deep into the beach. That meant that Venice was about a mile behind us. Then we lost Burke and the long-haired guy, while we maneuvered onto the ramp leading up to the pier. Foot traffic was as congested as the freeways at rush hour, and we got off our bikes and pushed them up the incline.

''I think she is on the carousel, her!'' Justine said happily, her eyes lighting up as the twinkling music of the calliope poured over us like peppermint syrup. We hurried into the quaint old merry-go-round building, with its turn-of-the-century turreted roof.

''No such luck,'' I said unconvincingly, as much under the spell of the scene and the sound as she was. Inside I stopped to stare at this garish ghost from my childhood. The horses were sparkling in new acrylic paint. They wore their bright new trappings proudly, nostrils flared as they seemed to sniff the ocean air, hooves suspended, waiting to paw impatiently at the sedate circular path they forever paced.

''Hey,'' I said softly. ''Hey and wow!''

Justine interrupted my reverie. "There's Burke. On the white horse."

"Holy Toledo—you're right!" The white horse was bobbing up and down, up and down. The guy with the long dark hair was on the horse beside her, watching her. "Hey, Burke, what do you think you're doing, anyway?" I yelled, and she turned, startled, and saw us.

"Hello—hello!" she called cheerfully, and I could have killed, killed. But the merry-go-round went on around, and we lost her for a minute. When the white horse reappeared, the music started to slow, and in a few more rounds the carousel stopped. The guy beside Burke hopped down, his hair swinging loosely, and reached up for her, grabbing her. It looked to me as though he was just trying to help her down.

Burke screamed. She screamed and screamed, and the guy split, on the run and out of sight. We never saw him again. The manager came tearing over, "law suit" written all over his white face.

"Miss, are you all right? What happened?"

Burke ran past him and straight out to the pier.

I ran after her, with Justine trailing. "Burke! Wait! What happened?"

"He touched me! He touched me!" she screamed, and some guys coming towards us grabbed *me*.

"Now just hold it, Jack. What'd you do to her?" They pinned my arms.

"Not him! Not him! Let him go!" Burke stopped suddenly, just ahead of us.

"You're sure, lady?"

She nodded frantically, and they let me go.

"Crazies," one of them said. "All over the place!"

Justine and I caught up with Burke, who had started to walk away fast.

"Come on, Burke—get your bike and let's go," I ordered.

"I can't ride home! I'm going to call Father! My bike's back at the merry-go-round! I don't want it any more! Oh, Maximilian, he grabbed me!" She started to cry, and then to run. There were too many people. We lost her.

"Her bike!" I said, making a fast U-turn and running back towards the carousel. "Come on!"

"Oh, Maximilian—she doesn't care about it! Why should we?" She had a point.

"She's unstrung," I shouted. "She'll be sorry, tomorrow!"

We found the bike, leaning against the back of the ticket office, inside the building.

"Let's chain it up with my lock, and we'll ride our bikes on home," I said reasonably.

"What is a chain, *cher?*" Justine said, just as reasonably. "If the bike is here very long, someone will cut the chain, Maximilian."

"Don't you think her dad will remember it when he comes to pick her up?"

"Maybe, and maybe not, Maximilian. *She* won't remember it." She had another point. As we wheeled Burke's bike towards the door, the manager came up to us.

"Are you friends of the red-haired young lady?"

"Yes. You could say so," I said. "Why?"

"Is she all right?" I could see the dollar signs.

"Sure. She just gets—nervous."

"You're sure she's okay? She should have filled out the form in the office."

"She's okay." I hoped my voice sounded more convincing than I felt. In my book, she was shaping up a real loony.

I unlocked our bikes while Justine held onto Burke's.

"So how you are going to do this, Maximilian? Ride two bikes like a circus man, hahn?" She watched me and the bikes anxiously.

"I don't know. But I think I can ride mine and guide hers alongside, except where there are too many people. Then I'll have to get off and walk both of them."

"You will be late to work, Maximilian, even if you don't fall off on the way home, and I think you will, *cher.*"

"Well, thanks a lot, Cherie. Here, take your bike." She was right, of course. I was a pretty good look-ma-no-hands rider, but all you needed was for two bikes just to touch, and somebody was going to hit the dirt. And I refused to be late for work. If I had to, I'd chain up Burke's bike along the way, highball on home, then call Mr. Lindstrom.

The proverbial blessing in disguise happened seconds later as we were threading our way through the mob at the foot of the ramp leading off the pier. A skater waltzed backwards right into me. The two bikes fell over, with me on top of them.

"You brainless bird!" I yelled. "Look what you've done!"

"Oh, Maximilian!" Justine screamed, pawing at the pileup.

"Hey, Maxie, it's me! You fell for me again! Ha ha ha!" I looked up. There was no mistaking that laugh.

"You jerk, Trinka Teitelbaum!" A dozen or so anonymous hands reached for me and pulled me out of the tangle. I straightened a few spokes while Justine hysterically explained our problems to Trinka, who had finally stopped laughing.

I stood up, eyeing the terrible Teitelbaum. "I've got an idea."

"I've got the same one," Trinka said. She stooped to take off her skates. "I keep telling you, Maxie, we're made for each other!" She took Burke's bike, and dumped her skate shoes into the basket. Then she pulled at the fake mink bikini. "No use, it won't stretch," she said ruefully.

"Not to worry," I said. "This bike's the luxury model. You'll wallow in splendor in that sheepskin seat cover."

When we dropped off the bike at the Lindstroms', Mrs. L glanced at Trinka disapprovingly, her green eyes narrowed. "I'm afraid you can't come in. Burke is under sedation."

★ ★ 8

I'd been thinking about Burke all day Sunday, and I was getting madder by the minute. So I stopped her on Monday morning by the bottle-brush tree on the way to English Lit.

"Hold it, Burke. You're going to level with me—now. What's with that screaming scene Saturday, and who was that street dude you picked up? Holy Sacramento, Venice is the native habitat of the West Coast's wackos! He could've raped you and tossed you into the drink at the end of the pier!"

She smiled serenely. "I think you're overreacting, Maximilian."

"Oh, you do, hah! Well, I think you should see a shrink! You may be a candidate for Mensa, and you're sure an okay fiddler if you've gone up in lights at the Music Center—but in my book you're bonkers!" I stared hard at her, not missing the fact that today she was the hands-down Miss Svelte California in narrow-wale cords that looked like white velvet and a white cashmere turtleneck. She wore a king's cache of little gold chains, and had tied her hair at the crown with a gold cord.

She said radiantly, "Maximilian, I can't thank you and the girls enough for bringing my bicycle home. One of you should have taken the twenty dollars Angelica offered you for your trouble.''

I cooled off. ''What! For doing a favor for a—friend?'' Was she? I hadn't decided. ''Now quit stalling and tell me what that screaming on the carousel was all about. You owe me one, Burke.''

''You sound just like my father, Maximilian.''

''So what did you tell *him?*''

''I told him a friendly boy came up to me when I was unlocking my bike and asked if I had seen the beautifully restored Philadelphia Toboggan Company carousel on the Santa Monica Pier. We were instantly compatible. Now how did he know that merry-go-rounds are a particular passion of mine?''

''A likely story!'' I was flabbergasted at her naïveté. ''You may have conned your dad, but I'm not buying it. You didn't need to draft a hophead, you know. The whole setup scared us, Justine and me. Why didn't you wait for *us?* We could have gone with you if you just *had* to see a merry-go-round!''

''Maximilian, why are you so upset? I had no idea when you would be ready to go home! It was—serendipity. That boy knew a great deal about carousels. He wants to own a genuine Charles Looff horse some day. It's too bad that collectors are buying the old machines just to remove the animals, though, isn't it? But I suppose it's the only way, in the long run, to preserve the beautiful carvings . . .''

''So,'' I interrupted her ravings, ''if you two were up on such a high intellectual plane, how come the Victorian hysterics?''

She turned away, shrugging. ''He touched me.''

''So he touched you! You're lucky that's *all* he did! What on earth did you expect, Little Miss Muffet?'' I couldn't get over it—she was born too late. She belonged in the seventeenth century with Marvell's coy mistress.

"I'm not going to talk about it any more." She looked at me with cool violet eyes.

I resisted the urge to shake her. "You better talk about it soon, Burke. To a shrink—or somebody. As I said, in my book you're looking pretty flaky, and I think you need help. What's this all about, this don't-touch-me bit?"

She started walking. Her voice was low. "I know I owe you one, Maximilian. But I can't tell you. It's just that— something happened—in my childhood. That's what they always say, isn't it!"

"That's what *you* say! Things happen to everybody. Not everybody screams their heads off ever after. Come on, we're about to be late to class."

"Just a second. You said I owed you one. I really owe you more than one, Maximilian. Will you come to my 'Evening with Burke Lindstrom' next Sunday? It's at six o'clock, with a champagne buffet afterwards. I'm giving a preview of my performance with the Houston Symphony in April. But don't expect a full orchestra this time. It'll be just me and my piano accompanist." She paused. "Will you come? I'm going to ask Justine, too."

I didn't think I'd like her "Evening," but the champagne buffet grabbed me. What heady *haute cuisine* would grace the Lindstroms' festive board—hummingbird fillets? Then there was the dream car, the Boat-Tail Auburn . . . I nodded. "Yes. Thanks."

I chained my bike to the same familiar light post in front of the Lindstroms' condo, and unclamped my hostess gift from the rack behind the bike seat. I'd brought a can of

Hawaiian macadamia nuts with a frilly white bow on top in a "plain brown wrapper," a lunch sack, as though it had been porno. The gift and the bow were Mom's idea. She'd been adamant, as they say. The *color* of the bow was *my* idea. Mom had wanted blue, to match the can. But I could stand to score a few points with the white-winged creature, Burke's mom. As it turned out, a maid answered the door and took the can of nuts and that was the last I ever saw of it.

White folding chairs filled the living room—each one had ABBEY RENTS printed across the back. I picked one at the rear, not too far from the door, as people do in church, the better to split at top speed with the final "amen."

I felt like an orphan, unclaimed by anyone but the Lindstroms, and Mr. and Mrs. were pretty preocccupied with the Beautiful People in their Dior dresses and Hong Kong hand-tailored suits. I longed for my Louisiana lovely, but Aunt Celeste had thirty-dollar-per tickets for the ballet at the Music Center and wasn't about to let Justine off the hook.

I blended into the upward-mobility scene pretty well in my navy blazer and new gray pants. Dad gave me the pick of his shirts and ties, and I had chosen an Oxford-blue shirt and a "classical" tie, as Mom called it, dark maroon with a modest, thin blue stripe. Dad's shirt wasn't exactly a custom fit, but unless I took off my jacket, nobody could tell it was too wide in the body and an inch too short in the sleeves.

I looked around for Burke, standing up to spot hair matching mine. I didn't see her. She was probably saving her strength.

Somebody handed me a Xeroxed program. I studied it while the conversation rippled around me, the "island" that no man is supposed to be, according to John Donne, anyway. (He was the subject of my special report for Mr. Nielson.)

An Evening with Burke Lindstrom

featuring the soloist in a preview of her performance
on April 11 with the Houston Symphony Orchestra

The D Minor Concerto for Violin, Op. 47 . . . . . . Sibelius
Zapateado . . . . Sarasate

Miss Lindstrom will be accompanied at the piano
by Mr. David Norwood

It turned out Mr. David Norwood was a welcome contrast to the Lindstroms' whiteout. He was a black guy in a black suit, with bow tie and tails that I'd never seen outside the late-lates on TV; you know, the dude in the top hat who comes tap dancing down the spiral stairway to the bevy of beauties in feather dusters. I started to laugh, and had to cover my mouth to imitate a cough.

Something finally happened. Mr. David Norwood sat down at the giant gold piano, which had been pushed to one end of the room, flapping his tails out behind the white-fur upholstered bench. People started choosing seats around the room until they were all taken, and some guests had to really cozy up to each other on the mile-long sofa. Suddenly somebody hit the noise off-button and the room turned as quiet as our house on New Year's Eve. I felt like holding my breath. Breathing was noisy.

Then Burke glided in from somewhere, and stood at the bend in the Steinway. She was slightly smashing in a long, fluffy white dress with thin shoulder straps. She wore a big, glittering ornament on her belt—real diamonds?—and a matching tiara, like royalty. She nodded towards the pianist and he immediately struck a note. She tuned the plum-colored fiddle, then stood up straight, looking a head taller than she really was.

After staring past all of us for a minute, she raised the violin up under her chin, her bow at the ready. But the first one to play was Mr. David Norwood, who got in a few licks before Burke chimed in.

This was it. The concerto. I'd heard of them. I sat back and decided to put imaginary pictures to the music. Snow was falling in distant mountains; once in a while the soft flurries turned to slivers of sleet. Then things got rougher: rushing rivers and rumbling cataracts and deep gorges. I stared in amazement at Burke.

She was swooping and swaying and tearing into that fiddle like a mad woman, working harder than *I* ever had in my life. Only an iron spine could be keeping her from collapsing.

At one point I thought the concerto was winding down, but it suddenly swept into a Gypsy camp with a wild abandonment that made you want to dance naked with the Gypsy king's raven-haired daughter. Then it rushed up Norway's fjords and scaled the cliffs to strike sparks from the North Star. The flashing lights of the aurora borealis consumed the whole world and the music ended. It was a few seconds before I breathed again.

Suddenly everybody in the room jumped up. The hand-clapping was deafening. I was on my feet too and was glad when the bravos started. "Bravo, Burke! Bravo! Bravo!" It was good to let off steam.

Burke smiled distantly and inclined her head. Finally she raised her violin and bow, and the room quieted again as everyone sat down. She waited for the rustling to die down, then she and Mr. David Norwood struck up the Zapateado, a fast number that had me tapping my feet on the thick white carpet. It occurred to me it was lucky Dad browbeat me into doing a good job on my shoes; there wasn't a chance of Renu-Shu messing up the carpet.

When the final huzzas and applause simmered down, Burke did her head-bowing routine again, and gestured to Mr. David Norwood, who stood up and bowed from the waist. When the bowing bit was over, Burke put her fiddle and bow in a case, and was immediately swallowed up by the Beautiful People.

I wondered where the food was. I could smell it, and I was ready. I was moving through the chairs towards the dining room, to have a look, when I bumped into a guy maybe two or three years older than I was. And light-years different looking—a little taller than my six two, with wavy blonde hair that stayed in place the way hair should, and a suit that whispered "big bucks."

"Oh, sorry," he said, and held out his hand. "I'm Langford Oliveras Van Alston." I almost expected him to hand me his business card.

"Hi." I looked at him curiously. "Say, where did that *Oliveras* come from? It sounds Chic—er, Mexi—Latino." I wished for once I was one of those smooth dudes, instead of what Mom calls a "diamond in the rough."

"It's Spanish. We're one of the old land-grant families. You've heard of Rancho Oliveras? That's still our Malibu spread, down from seventy-five thousand acres in 1835 to three hundred twenty today. Call me Lanny. And you? Have we met before?"

"No. I'm Maximilian Merriwether Murphy, of the Belview Beach landed gentry, since 1913. Call me Maximilian." I grinned, and we shook hands.

"Right, Maximilian. Say, do you think the food's on yet? I'm starved. I couldn't get near Burke, so I decided to check out the buffet."

"My strategy too." I liked the guy. I remembered that Burke didn't. "Have you known Burke long?"

"Almost all our lives. Since we were little kids. Our mothers met when they were both docents at the art museum."

That sounded a little too rich for my blood. "She's a good violinist," I said, feeling on safe ground there.

"One of the top two or three in the world, on her way to being *the* best," Lanny said. "And unquestionably the prettiest."

I didn't think she was all *that* pretty—not pretty like Justine, but, well, smashing, maybe. But this was *un*safe ground. "You think a lot of her," I pried, living dangerously.

"Sure. I'm in love with her. Have been ever since she fell down at my birthday party—I was eight, I think—and I laughed at her. So she threw a piece of cake in my face. I'm a sucker for a spunky woman!"

We squeezed past the last hand-tailored suit and silk dress and were finally in the dining room.

"Hey, hey!" It was awe-inspiring. A fountain encircled by flowers stood in the center of the huge table, spouting something that smelled like champagne.

"Aha—champagne," Lanny confirmed, taking two glasses and filling them. He handed me one. I hadn't had champagne since my cousin's wedding; I was only twelve, and he had slipped me a few sips. I had felt heady with sophistication. Booze was a no-no at the Murphys' digs.

"Thanks," I said.

Two maids in black uniforms with frilly white caps were

making quick trips to and from the kitchen, bearing heaping platters. I was in the last throes of starvation, but I held back. Mom would have been proud of me.

Lanny said, "Let's dig in." He took a plate and started loading it, so I followed. We helped ourselves to the tail and a couple of slices off the rump of a baked ham shaped like a piglet, with a baked apple in its mouth. A silver tray next to it held black stuff molded into a flower shape. I was game. It must be edible. I sliced off a couple of chunks.

"You must like paté and truffles," Lanny observed.

"Truffles? Oh, right. My favorite," I lied. Truffles?

"I loathe them—nasty black fungus. And paté—the liver from some poor tortured goose. Disgusting. Now this chicken Kiev here—that's different. Take plenty. You'll wish you had."

I piled wild rice over the fungus to disguise it, then went on to Swedish meatballs and hot German potato salad. I couldn't pass up the tomatoes stuffed with shrimp, and started double-decking. My culinary guide identified eastern crab and lobster aspic, and I recognized on my own the vegetable and fruit platters, and nut-covered cheese balls. I triple-decked the hot rolls.

"We'll get the sherbets later," Lanny said. We had just filled our glasses with champagne again and were on our way out of the dining room when Burke came in, trailing a clutch of admiring friends.

Lanny set down his plate and glass on the edge of the table and tried to push through to her, saying, "Darling, you were quite *wonderful*." But she avoided him adroitly and came straight to me.

"Maximilian, you *did* come!" I was surprised, and flattered, that she noticed Mr. Nobody Murphy.

What to say? "You did—really okay, Burke," I mumbled. It had come out all wrong. She was great, terrific. Everybody said so.

She smiled a little. "Thank you. Please, everybody, do enjoy the buffet." She was swallowed up again in a wave of admirers.

Lanny retrieved his plate and glass. "Well, I've lost her again. Let's go in here, Maximilian—the study. Breathing room." I followed him. It was a relief to be on home ground. After that session with Andrew Marvell, I felt as though I had a half-interest in the study. We sat in style at the big table, in the white leather chairs.

"How about trading places?" Lanny said in a quiet voice. I must have looked as surprised as I felt. These chairs all looked alike to me! "No, no—I don't mean here at the table! I mean, how about you being Langford Oliveras Van Alston of Rancho Oliveras, and let me be Maximilian Murphy of Belview Beach? I think she'd like me much better."

"So why *doesn't* she like you better?" He seemed like an okay guy to me.

Lanny laughed, breaking the heavy scene. "That's what I keep asking myself, how can she resist me! But she manages quite well! Where did you meet her, Maximilian?"

"We're school friends—Mira Vista High School."

"Very good," he said. "Of course she has no business in a public school. She's much too gifted. She belongs at Juilliard, or the Curtis Institute—the great conservatories." He glanced up from his plate and smiled. "Sorry, no offense. Nothing personal, Maximilian."

"Okay." I decided to level. "But maybe you're right. Maybe she *doesn't* belong at M.V. High. She gets up-tight over every little ordinary thing, like a dinky English report. And she can't stand people touching her. It's weird."

"She can't stand *men* touching her." Lanny glanced at me curiously. "How good a friend *are* you?"

I'd said the wrong thing for sure. I felt my ears burning, and the harder I tried to keep my cool, the hotter I felt. I bent over my plate, scooping up the last truffle.

"Casual. School friends." I tried to fix it up. "She invited me tonight, I think, because I've helped her with some homework."

"I see." Lanny was smiling again. "She's a perfectionist, you see. Everything in her life has to be *exactly* right."

"I think she needs help—about people touching her." I got back to that, doggedly.

"Men touching her." He finished off his aspic. "But she'll outgrow that. I'll wait for her."

The door, which was just half-closed, swung open, and an elegant woman walked in, not too tall, slim, with dark hair twisted into a loose knot at the back of her head. She was wearing something beige and "understated," as they say, and obviously expensive.

"Oh, there you are, Langford. I've been looking for you."

"Mother, this is Maximilian Murphy, a school friend of Burke's. My mother, Ann-Oliveras Van Alston."

I silently thanked Dad for whacking my bottom with a rolled-up newspaper every time I forgot to stand up when a lady came into the room, when I was a little kid. Of course Mom didn't count; she was in and out of the room all the time and I would have looked like a Jack-in-the-box. But Grandma counted, as I found out when I had trouble sitting down one night—Dad had rolled up the Sunday *Times*. So now I automatically jumped to my feet. The lady graciously held out her hand. I wondered briefly if I was supposed to kiss it. I settled for a brief shake, and a how-do-you-do.

"Hello, Maximilian. Langford, do be a dear and get your poor old mother a glass of champagne, would you?" She sat down, smiling.

"I'll take your glass along too, Maximilian." Lanny gathered the three glasses and left, and I panicked. What do you say to an elegant lady, one who is obviously not poor, and not all that old, either? Well, I found out that one thing that makes a lady elegant, is that *she* knows what to say.

"I'm so sorry that Raoul, my husband, couldn't be here tonight. He adores Burke—we both do. And hearing her play is the treat of the year for all of us. Alas, he's gone off to Chicago on business. But you can be sure we *all* hope to be present in Houston for Burke's concert. Will you be there, Maximilian?"

"Why, ah—maybe." Maybe not, too.

"Oh, you must! Burke is so fantastic. In fact, the Lindstroms are a remarkable family. Carter's a marvelous pragmatist, a true Jamesian. Angelica's talent is creative. And Burke is an interpretive genius, wouldn't you say, Maximilian?"

I was evidently expected to say something. "Yes, ma'am. That is, er, right."

She smiled. "But of course it's the *young* people you are interested in. We'll start with Langford. He's majoring in biology at Stanford, with a goal of postgraduate work in urban entomology—biological controls, such as the parasitic wasps that are the natural enemies of some cockroaches."

"Burke will be glad to hear about that," I said. "She hates cockroaches."

She laughed. "She has lots of company, I'm sure! Our daughter Samantha is a business major at Smith. She'll be a vice-president in our business. Now what are your goals, dear?"

I was taken aback, as they say. This was a pretty swift survey, and I didn't exactly want to discuss my personal affairs with a stranger, even one as elegant as Mrs. Van Alston. I made it brief. "I'm a mime."

"A mime! Pantomime?"

That was the key that started my motor. "That's close. Actually *Mime* with a capital *M* means the modern French techniques developed by Marcel Marceau's teacher, Etienne Decroux, as applied to the art of speaking through body language. *Mime* with a little *m* is the actor. *Pantomime* is using Mime techniques and styles to tell a story." I noticed it was getting easier to talk.

"How well-informed you are, Maximilian! By an interesting coincidence, a group I'm working very closely with is planning to hire a young mime to work with autistic children, and others that are psychologically damaged . . ."

"Yes, ma'am," I anticipated her, having heard the pitch before, "Burke told me. The Damaged Children's Foundation."

"Exactly. You might want to apply for an interview and tryout . . ."

Before I could protest politely, Lanny came in, carrying three glasses.

"So, Maximilian, Mother has been giving you one of her famous lectures, no doubt. I can tell you it isn't easy living with a do-gooder and art connoisseur. However, she *is* particularly fine on Periclean Athens."

"We weren't talking about art, dear. But I do readily

confess to loving that second phase of classical Greek art. You see, Periclean architecture and sculpture reached out towards life as a whole, rather the opposite of Olympian art of the first period, which tragically and narrowly stressed the depths of the human soul . . .''

Lanny said quickly, "Champagne. Mother, your glass is on the right." She took it, carefully. "And yours, Maximilian." I was beginning to get into this man-of-the-world stuff. I lifted my glass just as high as Lanny's. He said, "To my darling, the most beautiful and the best!" I was glad he had never seen Justine.

"I'll drink to that," I said glibly.

"I'm surprised there was any champagne left," Mrs. Van Alston said, sipping hers. "I couldn't get near the fountain."

"Well, the hospitable Lindstrom fountain will never run dry, unlike the pools at Versailles. How gross to see those cut-off creatures rising out of cement!" He paused, and I drained my glass. "Easy there, Maximilian. Champagne is a time bomb, you know."

"I'm okay—full of that great dinner," I said expansively.

"Food. I'm starving," Mrs. Van Alston said, getting up.

"Shall I get you something, Mother?"

"No thanks, dear. I'm going to find Abraham Aaronson first. I'm so glad he could come. He's so *very* fond of Burke. In fact, I wonder how he can be objective when he reviews her. He *has* been known to give her a less than perfect score."

"That's why he's so respected, I suspect," Lanny said. "I think he's retirement age, but the *Times* will never let him go if they can help it."

One of the maids in the frilly caps came in the door. She was carrying a champagne bottle wrapped in a fancy towel. "Please?" She held out the bottle.

"No, thank you," Ann-Oliveras Van Alston said. "Nice to have talked with you, Maximilian." She left.

Lanny said to the maid, "No more, thanks. I'm going to see if I can get anywhere near Burke." He left.

"Well, just a little, thanks," I said, and the maid poured a glassful. I sat down on the love seat facing the Swedish fireplace. It was getting a little hard to stand.

★ ★ *9*

Voices woke me. I was surprised to find myself folded up neatly in something the size of a suitcase. My head felt as if it had been hit by a flatiron. This was it—I was dead, at worst; or dying, at best. Gradually, a large, threatening white object floated into focus. Ah, the Swedish fireplace! Fragments of my mind groped for details. The last I remembered, I was on my feet in the study, soberly swigging a glass of bubbly. Inexplicably I was now lying on the love seat, in Marcel Marceau's Old-Man-Dying position. A black hole had swallowed moments? minutes? hours?

"My dear child," a deep voice cut into my consciousness, "what are your plans?"

"Why, to go on concertizing, I suppose." It was Burke, clear and coherent. I held my breath.

I was an eavesdropper—an open mike—a human bug. The thought appalled me, as they say.

"Well, you must not 'suppose,' my dear. When are you entering the conservatory, and which one?" The deep voice again.

"Why, I have no plans for the conservatory—at present, Mr. Aaronson."

I concentrated on silent breathing.

"And why not? Are you already so satisfied with your performance? At age what, sixteen?" He sounded like a nice guy, but he was way off base, in my book. Her performance had sounded great, to me.

"Sixteen, yes. And, no, I'm not at all satisfied. Heifetz' bowing in the Adagio has much greater clarity and brilliance than mine. I think I'm closer to Danielle Drake—she was only seventeen when she made that incredible recording of Sibelius' D Minor. I admire her, but I'd really rather follow the Russian school than the German. To play like Heifetz is my goal, Mr. Aaronson."

"I know, dear child. It is the goal of every violinist ever born since Heifetz. But there is only one Heifetz. There is only one Kreisler. And only one Danielle Drake—what a fine talent, but the child let her light go out years ago. She chose a happy life—marriage and children."

I froze at the words. I guess Burke did, too, because it was a minute before she said anything. Then her voice came out so low I could hardly hear her.

"Happiness to me is perfection. I will come as close to Heifetz as is possible in this world, I assure you, Mr. Aaronson."

"I'm sure you will, little Burke. But you will not *be* Jascha Heifetz. You will be Burke Lindstrom, and you will be a Burke Lindstrom the world will remember, not a copy of Heifetz. And that is exactly the point—why you *must* go to a conservatory. For that is where you will learn to develop your personal style, your signature. Technique you already have, my dear. But *style* must be perceived and developed in a young artist through the widest possible exposure to literature for the instrument and through the sensitivity and skill of master teachers. Be the original, Burke, not a Xerox copy, even if that were possible. You are giving the world Burke Lindstrom, and it is a great gift. You must keep on honing it to a fine perfection.''

I didn't hear Burke for a second or two, but I pictured her smiling graciously at his verbal applause, or humbly bowing her head to receive more. I was surprised when she said abruptly, "I am not happy wth the Adagio tonight."

"You didn't miss a note, child. Be happy with it.''

"No. Five bars into it, I realized my new D-string was stretching, and I had to compensate. I'm glad my mother isn't a technician—she would stop speaking to me for a week! But she only notices the obvious.''

My head was getting clearer by the minute, clear enough to make me aware of the necessity of keeping a very low profile.

"Stop speaking to you for a week, Burke? You mean that rhetorically, of course.''

"No,'' Burke said bluntly. "When she stops speaking to me, it is only to make me try harder for perfection in my work. But Mr. Aaronson, it's the cruelest thing . . .'' Her voice caught, and the next words were very low. "Harder than a bad review.''

There wasn't a sound for a minute or two. Then the deep voice said, "Here—my vest-pocket handkerchief is spotless. Please feel free.''

"Thank you.'' I barely heard it.

"I'm sorry I probed. Curiosity—a newspaperman's Achilles heel.'' He waited a beat. Then evidently his Achilles heel began kicking up again. "But since your mother's opinion is just that—a layman's opinion, and not professional criticism, it seems to me you should take it more philosophically, my dear. *All* parents yearn for perfect children, as they themselves were not, you know.''

"I want to please my mother." Her voice was still low.

"And your father?"

"He loves me, whatever I do. Father is my best friend."

"You are most fortunate to have a best friend. Not everyone has."

Burke's voice was coming out stronger. "Of course I have many friends in music, and a few casual friends at school. One of them is here tonight."

I stopped breathing again, momentarily.

"What school, Burke? I thought you were being educated by tutors."

"I was, until this semester. Then it seemed—best for me, to go to a public high school." Her voice trailed off.

"Best for you—why? How can you fit it in—the standardized curriculum, the daily classes—with your practicing, your concertizing? How is that *best* for you?"

"It's just that—I felt I was being funneled through a very, very narrow segment of life: the music world, with its brilliant but one-sided people, its insular interests. I guess I just wanted a taste of the flip side—the *real* world."

There was a deep laugh, then I heard the door swing open, followed by one of those stagy voices some women turn on and off like a spotlight. "So *there* you are, dear Abe! I thought I heard your famous laugh! Is Burke monopolizing you?" There was a familiar edge to the words; the winged one?

"No, rather the other way around, I'm afraid, Angelica." I was right. "I'm keeping Burke from all those handsome young men out there. Now I must run along. I have a review to write, you know, while it's fresh in my mind. Burke, dear child, you were quite wonderful tonight, as you must be aware—especially in the last movement. Yours was a passionate, a glittering interpretation."

There were the usual polite exclamation points. "You are so very kind . . . !" "So sorry you have to . . . ! "Your charming and gifted daughter . . . !" "Goodbye, and thank you . . . !"

After his fade-out, Mrs. Lindstrom sang out sweetly, "Oh, do stay here, Burke darling. Lanny's looking for you. I'll tell him you're in the library." I guess she left the door open. I could hear the steady patter of conversation under Burke's cry,

"Angelica . . . please!"

I tested one cramped knee, cautiously, hoping Burke wasn't looking my way. The knee was operational, and I eased it back up under my chin on top of the other one.

Lanny's voice faded in. "At last I've found you, darling! How about my building a fire in the fireplace? We could cozy up on the love seat." I suspected that suggestion would bring a strong reaction, but I shrank up like bacon on a hot griddle anyway, trying to make myself smaller.

Burke said on cue, "Don't bother, Lanny. It's time I joined the others in the living room."

"Now just a moment, love. I've brought you a little present, a recital gift."

"Lanny, I don't want any gifts from you! You *know* that!" I couldn't understand her. *I* never turned down anything. But I somehow felt sorry for her. There was something in her voice—maybe a sadness? Or a pleading—for what? Her own space, maybe. I stopped trying to sort it out. My head was throbbing.

"You aren't exactly consistent, sweetheart."

"That's unkind of you, Lanny! The piano, the Guarnerius Ann wants me to have—those are from your *parents*. Are you trying to make me feel obligated to *you?*" Her voice rose sharply. "You *know* they're helping other young artists, too!"

"That's *their* project. You're *mine,* darling. Let's unwrap this . . ." I heard the rustle of paper.

"Oh, Lanny—it's terribly expensive!"

"Nonsense. It's just an old, used Navajo necklace."

"Yes—an old, used *pawned* piece at least seventy-five-years old and worth a fortune!" Burke cried.

"The silver and turquoise become you, Lady Burke."

"But a squash-blossom necklace—of this size! Oh, it *is* lovely . . ." She sounded a little uncertain. "Lanny, where *did* you find it?"

"The Ganado trading post, in Arizona. Look under that layer of paper."

"Oh—not a bracelet, too!" Her voice was high-pitched, excited. "It's magnificent!"

Lanny said, "From the old Chinle post. Thunderbird Lodge."

Chinle! Ancestral home of our old Navajo rug! I almost sat up in my surprise, then thanked my head for being too heavy to lift.

Burke was saying sadly, "Oh, Lanny, they're *lovely!* But I can't possibly keep them. It was cruel to even show them to me . . ." Her voice trembled.

"Keep them, sweetheart. My parents paid the bill. I merely did the shopping. Now stop shaking your head no . . ."

"The whole subject is academic anyway. I can't wear jewelry when I'm playing. I know that's what you'd like, but it's quite impossible to do."

"Wear it when you're *not* playing, love. Wear it for Mother's sake. She'll love you for it."

There was a smile in Burke's voice when she said

softly, "I'll ask her, you may be sure of that. But frankly, I think you're improvising, Lanny."

"I've had a little practice."

There was a long moment of quiet. I was pining to peek, but there was nothing about my red hair that would blend into the white love seat, even if I could raise my head and unwind from my frozen fetal position.

Then came the explosion. I jumped at the sound of the muffled scream, followed by the hysterical words, "Oh, don't *touch* me! Leave me alone!" Followed by more muffled screams. I held my breath.

"You're going to have to get used to my kisses, darling. This isn't the first time, and it won't be the last."

"I *hate* you, Lanny Van Alston! Don't ever touch me again! And take your junk jewelry! If I have to pay for it, I don't want any part of it!" I heard the clank-clank of things thrown on the floor. It was another echo. Were women really all alike? The rich and famous Langford Van Alston and the poor and infamous Maximilian Merriwether Murphy . . . we were walking in each others' moccasins.

The door swung open with a bang, hitting the wall.

"I thought so! You're creating a scene—again!" The voice was reigned-in rage. "What has she done now, Lanny? And what's this, on the floor?"

"They fell off, Angelica," Lanny said casually. "I'll see to the catches. You know how old pieces are."

"They didn't fall off! I threw them down! They're *expensive*, Angelica. He thinks he can obligate me! Well, he can't!" Burke's voice was full of fury.

"Stop it, Burke." The tone had the hardness of marine varnish. "You don't know how stupid that sounds!" There was a pause. "Pick it up! Oh, thank you, Lanny—but *she* should have done it."

"It's from all of us, Angelica, you know that. Mother says these were always meant for Burke—so perfect with her auburn hair . . ."

"It's red! Fire-engine red!" Burke—hysterical.

Mrs. Lindstrom—tightly: "You are so very thoughtful, Lanny. Ann-Oliveras and Raoul, too—all of you, so very, very, considerate. The jewelry is beautiful." She paused. "Put it on, Burke. *Right now!*" There was iron in those two words.

"I'd better run," Lanny said quickly. "Mother's probably looking for me. She has a board meeting at eight o'clock in the morning—some arts council or other." His voice was fading. "Well done tonight, Burke . . . Beautiful evening, Angelica. Now I must find Carter . . ."

"In the dining room, seeing to the champagne. I'll be with you in a moment, Lanny. There's something I want to tell Burke . . ."

I wished they would all leave. Six feet two . . . wadded up on a little sofa just half that length. I heard a click, like a key turning in a lock, then the verbal bombs went off. I was caught in a shallow foxhole on the battlefield.

"I will *not* wear these, Angelica! I don't care what you say! He *kissed* me!" Burke's voice was shaking.

"You could do worse than be kissed by *the* Langford Oliveras Van Alston, my girl! You must know that he's the most sought-after young man in Los Angeles! What *is* wrong with you, Burke? Why do you act this way? Is there a reason?"

"Yes!" It was a shout. "There *is* a reason—but I won't tell you, Angelica! I won't tell you!"

"Have you told your father? I know you love him— more than you do me!" Her voice shook, and I gulped—I had thought she was stuffed with iron filings.

"No—I haven't told Father! I wouldn't want him to think of me as—dirty!" I sucked in my breath, glad that the sound was muffled by Mrs. Lindstrom's voice.

"Dirty! What on earth do you mean by that? What could possibly be so terrible that you couldn't tell your parents?" Her voice was tense, apprehensive. I was apprehensive, too, I found, when I finally let out my breath.

Burke was saying stridently, "Since when have you been easy for me to talk to, Angelica? All we ever do is—*shout* at one another!"

"Keep your voice down, Burke!" It was a loud command.

Burke, loudly: "See? It's always been like this—even when I was six years old!"

"Six years old? Why did you say that? Did this—awful thing—happen *that* long ago?"

"More than—half a lifetime ago! Why should you care now, you didn't care then! You were too busy starting a career to care about what happened to *me*—or *my* career! Even Father was too busy, but it wasn't *his* fault! He was working and getting his master's at the same time."

"Nothing is *ever* your father's fault, is it! Oh, Burke, why is there this terrible wall between us? Is this the price I have to pay for a life of my own? I just want to be my own person—like your father, like you! *Not* just the mother of the famous child prodigy Burke Lindstrom! Is that too much?" Mrs. Lindstrom's voice was shaking a little. "How would you like to be merely Angelica Lindstrom's anonymous daughter?" I couldn't imagine either one of them ever being anonymous, but I couldn't hear Burke's answer. Her mother went on, "Why can't you love me as much as you love your father, Burke? Why? I've done so much for you!"

"Yes, you have, Angelica!" Burke was coming on strong now. "You *made* me go to that terrible man, that music teacher—Stanislaus Janoff—forty-five minutes a week for one year, didn't you! You *made* me! I screamed and cried and you wouldn't *listen* to me!"

"I listened to your screaming and crying and made up my mind I wasn't going to raise a spoiled brat, Burke! That man was one of the most respected violin teachers in town! We were lucky to get him! You may not know it, but he had come out of the Moscow Conservatory, played violin in the great symphony orchestras of Europe . . ."

"And *you* may not know it, Angelica, but he also—played with—little girls! Oh—oh!" There was a gasp and the sound of a smothered cry. I almost fell off the love seat—she couldn't mean what I was thinking she meant. I eased my face into the love seat's down pillow to silence my breathing, but I couldn't do much about my heart's loud pounding.

"Burke!" Mrs. Lindstrom's exclamation came out like a sob. "Oh, darling! Are you telling me . . . No, surely, you would have said something before this . . ." Her voice trailed off.

"You didn't believe me—I *tried* to tell you! I told you he *touched* me—but not the way you and Father touched me, not that way at all! I *told* you! You don't believe me *now,* do you? Well, it doesn't matter—I never *meant* to tell you, ever!"

"*I* thought you meant he positioned your hands on the violin, Burke! Oh, I don't know what to believe! Darling, I love you—I want to understand you! Please don't shut me out!" She was *pleading* with Burke.

"You'll never understand me, Angelica! You don't now—and you didn't then! I trusted that man—because *you* had chosen him for me! I *trusted* him!'' I pushed my face deeper into the pillow.

"Oh, Burke, Burke! *I* trusted him! Why shouldn't I have? Ann-Oliveras recommended him to me—she thought he was a *wonderful* teacher. Samantha studied with him for two years! Oh, what did he *do* to you, Burke?''

"Ann-Oliveras cared enough about Samantha to sit through every lesson with her! Ann didn't dump Samantha to go shopping on Rodeo Drive!''

"Oh, darling, is that what you thought, poor baby? You can be sure I wouldn't have paid fifty dollars for forty-five minutes of baby-sitting! It's just that—I was starting the agency . . . There was *so* much to do . . . I was so terribly busy . . . and so tired! Burke, you've *got* to tell me—what he *did* . . .''

"He was so gentle—and kind! His hands were so gentle—when he felt me—all over! His hands—his gentle hands . . .''

Mrs. Lindstrom cried out, "Burke! Oh, no!''

A chill swept over me, and I had to *will* myself to control it before it shook the love seat. Please, Up There— don't let me give myself away now! What would it do to Burke—to know that an eavesdropper—someone she *knew* . . . ?

"Oh, he was so kind, Angelica!'' Burke rushed on in a high, triumphant voice. It was almost as though she was *whipping* her mother. "He always gave me a present—for playing our secret game! Yes, that's what he called it— 'our secret game'! Oh, you remember the presents, Angelica—little dolls, dressed in costumes . . .''

"Darling, darling, I thought they were little rewards for a good lesson! Oh, Burke!'' I thought I heard short, muffled sobs.

"You spanked me for throwing those dolls in the fireplace one night!" Her voice was getting higher. I waited, tense. "But you couldn't make me cry! And I laughed and laughed when you fished that shapeless black mess out of the fire!" Her voice broke, and she laughed crazily. I had to control my shivering again.

"Burke—oh, don't! Don't!"

"It's too late for you to put your arms around me now, Angelica!" She had stopped laughing, and her voice was cold. "You should have done that—ten years ago!"

"Burke, don't push me away! Let me try to make up— let your father and me . . ."

"No! Father is not to know! *Ever!* I am his *princess!* *Swear* to me, Angelica!"

"Darling, how *can* I? You are *our* precious daughter— you will *always* be your father's fairytale princess! *You* have done nothing wrong, Burke—you must not think that! *It's that man who was evil!* No wonder he left secretly, without telling a soul! You were probably not the *only* child he molested! And to think that after all these years . . . *you* are still suffering for *his* crimes! Oh, darling, now I can see it! I never . . . understood!" It was a torrent of words, engulfing the room.

Burke's voice was pure acid. "Don't be ridiculous, Angelica. It's more like you to play Medea than Juliet's mother. I am *not* suffering. I'm fine. I have everything I need or want." Her tone said "buzz off." I couldn't believe the sudden switch.

"You have *nothing!*" Mrs. Lindstrom's voice was shaking again. "If you aren't happy, you have *nothing!* Darling, we'll get the best psychiatrist . . . *Now* you can have help! Everything is going to be all right! It's just that I—didn't *know* . . ."

"If you force me to go to a psychiatrist, I'll lie to him, I swear to you, Angelica. I'm sorry, now—sorry I didn't go on—keeping 'our little secret'—to myself."

"Burke, you're closing the door on me—again! Oh, please, darling, let me help . . ." Her mother sounded frantic.

"I don't want any help! I just want to be left alone!"

"Darling, no! I'll never leave you alone again . . . I promise . . ."

Someone pounded on the door. Oh, no—someone else who might decide to sit on the love seat. I curled into a tighter ball.

Mrs. Lindstrom chirped cheerfully, "Smile, darling!" I heard the door open. "Oh, Carter! I've just been telling Burke how very proud I am of her."

"Yes, indeed, Princess. Everyone here tonight is proud of you." Mr. Lindstrom's calm voice was a welcome relief. "But they're all about ready to leave. I thought the two charming hostesses should put in an appearance. Burke—aren't you feeling well?"

Burke said brightly, "Oh, yes, Father! But I expect I'm getting a little tired."

"And with reason! What a tremendous performance my princess gave for us commoners tonight! Let's go, ladies."

Burke's mom said chattily, "Was there enough champagne, Carter?"

"Plenty, my love. What a lucky man I am—with a beautiful woman on each arm . . ." His voice faded out.

I didn't hear the door close. I was dying by inches, sure that I was locked permanently into fetal position on the Lindstroms' love seat. I waited tensely for a few minutes, but all I heard was the rise and fall of voices in the living

room. The room was quiet, for a change. I raised my head
with considerable effort. The coast was clear. I knew I had
to split; my parents had probably thrown out a dragnet by
now. I unfurled my legs, and tried standing—then fell back
with a thump. The room was moving around in stately
circles, like the merry-go-round. Come on, head! Let's go,
feet! Somehow I had to sneak outside . . . get a breath of
fresh air . . . get my bike. I willed myself into standing
position. My legs were made of rubber, but I took a few
practice steps, then managed to clear the library door. I
listened. There were distant voices, towards the front of
the condo. Good! I headed into the kitchen, where I knew
there was a rear door. Someone brushed by me carrying a
tray, which crashed to the vinyl brick floor.

"Maximilian!" Burke's dad.

"Uh—sorry, sir, Mr. Lindstrom. What a—mess! Uh—
sorry." I stooped, with some difficulty—the room was still
doing its slow dance—and started scooping up sand-
wiches.

"Oh, never mind that, son. The maids are still here
. . ." The two girls in the frilly caps came rushing up,
clucking, "Oh, my, oh, my!"

"Where have you been, Maximilian?" We stepped aside
while the maids got to work. "Your parents called a while
back, and I told them I supposed you were on your way
home. I hadn't seen you around. Where were you?"

"Uh, resting, sir. In a chair, sort of hidden behind the
piano," I improvised. I hoped I wasn't going to get caught
in that "tangled web we weave when first we practice to
deceive," as Mom puts it. I leveled. "Afraid I overdid the
champagne a little, sir."

He laughed. "You do look on the pale side. Tricky stuff,

champagne. Well, go call your parents, Maximilian. The phone's on the wall there. Tell them you're okay, and I'm driving you right home.''

I nearly panicked. At that point I felt perilously close to losing my truffles, and I didn't want it to happen in the white Auburn phaeton.

"That's great of you, sir, but I'd just have to walk back to get my bike tomorrow.''

"Either way, son. But call home now.''

My father answered, and was *not* overjoyed about the hour—eleven o'clock. "On the double, Max! You hear me?''

I heard him all the way home through slightly ringing ears. When I finally tottered in the door, pausing to lean against the jamb, he roared, "So you've been drinking!''

I thought about lying, but the feeling passed quickly. My father could spot a lie at a hundred yards. "Uh—yes, sir. A little champagne, was all. Everybody was drinking it.''

"Everybody's cheating on welfare, too! In this house, nobody drinks booze, you got that, Max? *No booze!''* He was pulling off his belt. "I haven't found that old razor strop yet, but in the meantime . . . bend over!''

"Hey, Dad! You can't be serious! Hey, I'm sixteen— I'm almost six two—and I'm—I'm—sick!'' My hand flew to my mouth. The whole house was spinning like a top. I ran for the bathroom.

I could hear Dad laughing and dancing on my grave. "Learn anything?'' he shouted.

I just barely managed, "Yes—sir,'' before slamming the bathroom door.

"By the way, Max . . .'' He was instantly standing in the hall outside the door. "The UCLA Catalog came yesterday. I sent for it for you. It's never too early to start planning your Bruin career! Keep those grades up, you hear me, Max?''

Murphy's Law—in the flesh.

"Mox, Mama and me—we're movin' again." The Rabbit was as usual ahead of me as we charged straight down the sand hill. It was six-thirty in the morning, three days after Burke Lindstrom's incredible "Evening," and pewter-gray cold unless you were trying to break a four-minute mile.

"How so?" I projected, taking Mile-High Mulligan leaps down the steep dune. When I was a little kid, I'd run down this hill in seven-league boots, flapping my arms. It was the closest I'd ever come to flying.

"Because the border guys made a sweep, Mox. Of the beach restaurants. Of Paco's. Paco saw those guys comin' and pushed us wetbacks out the back door. Those guys must've thought Paco runs Paco's all by hisself." The Rabbit chuckled. "They sat down at the counter and they order' the Super-Sof' Tacos, and Paco he had to cook like hell, Mox. Paco don' like those INS guys!" The words faded as the distance between us lengthened.

"So are you still working for Paco, Rabbit?" I called. I'd catch him if the downhill would just hold out.

"Sure, Mox. But Mama an' me, we want to throw those guys off our trail. Now we live with Cousin Mario, but I will still come to Mira Vista."

I was losing contact. I raised my voice. "Rabbit, are

you signed up for the Kola King yet?'' The marathon was coming on fast.

The Rabbit turned and flashed a grin at me. "No. You an' me, we're goin' to sign up together. How much, Mox?''

He waited for me. "Five dollars,'' I puffed. "Nine, if you want the T-shirt.''

"Sure, Mox. Can you loan me?'' We loped off together, on the flatland again.

"Well, hey, Rabbit! You're working too!'' I protested. "How come you can't come up with nine bucks?'' I planned to preserve my poke against all encroachments.

"Well, Mox—there's all those kids in Creel. And you know, they want to get out of Creel sometime.''

"What kids?'' We were on the home stretch.

"My brothers an' sisters—maybe seven, eight kids! An' my papa, he don' do all that good, farmin' that little patch of mountain and makin' fiddles to trade at the store.''

"Your father makes fiddles—no kidding?''

"For sure, Mox! The best, around Copper Canyon! See you at school!'' He took a right turn and I went straight ahead.

"Ciao, Rabbit.'' Friendship had its price—nine bucks.

As usual after a run, I came home with the appetite of a killer whale. I grabbed the entertainment section as soon as I sat down at the table; our family is the last one in Belview Beach that enforces sit-down breakfasts.

"Here it is,'' I said, getting a firm handle on my excitement. Color me green! Burke Lindstrom . . . not only in lights at the Music Center, but in print in the prestigious *Times!* I clumsily folded the paper, with "Music Notes'' in full view. "Burke's review—that program I went to at her house."

"Read it, dear," Mom said, looking up from the business section.

"Okay. 'Capsule Comments on Last Weekend's Events, by Abraham Aaronson.' He was there, at the Lindstroms." I'd rubbed elbows, as they say, with the power of the press.

Dad said absently, "Yes, go on." He was consuming the sports section along with his scrambled eggs.

"Okay. 'Burke Lindstrom, Wunderkind of the music world' . . ."

"That means wonder-child—child prodigy," Dad said, showing off the German he had taken in college to get an engineering degree.

"Okay . . . 'of the music world, did it again at one of her famous private performances, "An Evening with Burke Lindstrom," Sunday in Belview Beach. The sixteen-year-old violinist gave a preview of the program she will present with the Houston Symphony in April. The nuances of her rendition of the technically challenging Sibelius Violin Concerto in D Minor were remarkable in sophistication, intonation, power, and clarity and gave proof not only of her mature musicality but of an amazing physical stamina. A romanticist, she swept into her encore, the Zapateado by Sarasate, with appropriate abandon. David Norwood accompanied at the piano. The performance augers well for Houston.' Unquote."

"Well! That young girl has it made," Mom said, hurrying in from the kitchen with a platter of pancakes. I flashed back to that mother-daughter scene in the library, and winced. "How fortunate she is—sixteen, and already famous!" She paid her dues, Mom.

"We'll have to catch her act at the Music Center some-time," Dad said, going back to the sports page. "And here's something else we'll have to catch, Maximilian—UCLA track and field this season. You might pick up some pointers on running. You'd like that, wouldn't you?"

"Yeah, I guess so."

"Is that all you have to say—'yeah, I guess so'?"

"I guess so, Dad." UCLA, again.

"Max! One more time and you leave the table!" We were all quiet a minute, except for Mom, who was humming "By the Old Pacific's Rolling Waters," an old UCLA song. Dad glanced up. "Max, save next Sunday after church. I'm taking you up to the campus, let you look around."

"Dad, I know UCLA like the back of my hand. Mom took me to *years* of junior programs there."

"Well, several seasons, anyway. That *was* great fun, wasn't it, dear?" Mom said.

"Yeah, Mom." Actually, it *had* been fun. It was real theater, even if it had been scaled down for kids. *I* had been a kid. I turned to Dad. "I don't know, Dad. I sort of had plans for Sunday—*after* the chores, of course." I took two more pancakes and drowned them in syrup. I *didn't* have any plans, except for the usual Sunday fifteen-mile run—but I'd sure work up some fast.

"Of *course* after your chores, son. You won't get out of those. This time it's windows to wash, but just your own room. That's not too tough, and will give us most of Sunday afternoon at UCLA."

"Windows! Come on, Dad, it's going to rain again!" I hated doing windows. No matter how great they looked at the time, the next morning they acquired glaring smears that never passed muster, and I had to do them again.

"We'll drop into Bear Wear in the student store," Dad steamrolled on. "Thought you could use a Bruin sweat suit, son—get into the blue and gold right now! No sense in waiting."

"Uh—I don't think so, Dad. I have an okay sweat suit. But I get so hot running I hardly ever wear it. I don't need another one I won't wear."

"Right. We'll get you a UCLA T-shirt and running shorts, then. How about a UCLA visor? They're pretty sharp looking! We'll have a great time, Max—just you and me!"

"Thanks a heap," Mom said.

"You want to come, Annie?" Dad pushed back his chair and got up.

"Of course not. I merely want to be *invited*. As a matter of fact, I'll have a glorious time here all by myself. I think I'll get a box of chocolates and pig out on the sofa all afternoon."

"Very funny, Annie. So come along, we don't care, do we, Max?"

"I—can't go, Dad." I made big stage business of helping myself to more sausages. "Sorry," I added contritely, catching a glimpse of Dad's face. "Good breakfast, Mom."

Mom shot me a laser-beam look. "This isn't your Sunday at the Inner-City Playhouse, is it, dear?"

"Of course it isn't. That's another two weeks," Dad said, scowling. "What's the matter, boy? All this running you're doing, this mime nonsense, all this skirt-chasing— interfering with your school work, isn't it! Are your grades down—is that it?"

"No, Dad—that isn't it." I stuffed my mouth with two link sausages, hoping that'd save me from further conversation.

"He simply doesn't want to go, Quentin. Why don't you just leave it at that?" Mom said.

"No! He's going to tell me *why*—right now. Swallow that mouthful and *talk,* Max. That's an order!"

I swallowed and took a gulp of air. Now was as bad a time as any. I had a go at it—the truth, *almost* the whole truth.

"The fact is, Dad—I'm not going to UCLA. So I don't want you to get your hopes up. It wouldn't be *honest*— my parading around in Bear Wear." It wasn't honest my not mentioning right now, the signatures I'd need to leave school, either.

I tensed for the usual explosion, and it came on schedule. "What! I knew it! Your grades are slipping! Well, you'll stop all this busy stuff as of *right now,* including that puny gas-station job! You're going to get back on the right track—plenty of rest, plenty of study—we'll get you a tutor this summer! What's the problem, Max, English, math?"

"I'm making *A*'s in English, Dad. I guess I'm a *B* in math. The problem is—well, I'm going to take the California Proficiency Test so I can quit school this June. I've met all my high-school requirements." I looked down at my plate and made a full-time job of mashing a bite of egg into my fork tines.

"Max . . . you're—*quitting* school?" Mom's shocked voice quavered.

"What!" Dad's roar overlapped Mom's half-whisper. "California Proficiency Test my Aunt Garbage! You haven't met your *college* requirements, I know *that* for a fact! What's this all about—and it better be good, boy!"

I took a big gulp of courage. "You're right, Dad. I haven't met college requirements because I'm not going to college. It's not all that big a deal. I'll get a Certificate of Proficiency instead of a diploma, is all.''

Dad's face was fiery red. "Is all!" he mimicked in a loud, squeaky voice. Now I could feel *my* face warming up. "Is *everything*, you young imbecile!" he shouted.

Mom looked ready to cry. "Oh, Max, Max—all my dreams . . .''

"But they weren't *my* dreams, Mom!" All the same, I could feel myself slipping into a guilt trip. "Hey, there's nothing wrong with a certificate—I'm not exactly a drop-out!''

"There's nothing wrong with digging ditches, either— if you can *get* one of those jobs!" Dad stood looming over me. "But in case you haven't noticed, they're being phased out! Ever hear of high tech? I'm getting in touch with your principal today! You shape up *right now* or I'm putting you in military school *tomorrow!*''

I looked up. Then I stood up. I faced him. "Dad, you're going to have to know this sometime. I'm getting into my career this summer. Maybe later I'll go on to college. But I've got to do it my way.''

"*Your* way! What do you know—a sixteen-year-old wet-behind-the-ears kid! What're you going to do for money, wash dishes at the Steak Space?" He grabbed me by the shoulders and gave me a hard shake.

"I'm a *mime!*" I chattered. "I've already got jobs lined up at the Village Mall! I'll be able to pay for my board and room!''

"Well you won't pay it *here*," Dad shouted. "If you quit school, you'll jolly well get yourself declared an emancipated minor and clear out of here!''

"Now, Quentin," Mom said, laying a hand on his arm. "Let's not issue any ultimatums. We're all too upset. Let's just calm down now and get on with the day." She looked me in the eye. "Maximilian, you are to go with your father on Sunday—to UCLA."

"Well—okay, Mom. But no Bear Wear." I surprised myself with my unaccustomed meekness. Mom didn't issue many orders, but when she did they carried the authority of a General of the Armies.

"Quentin dear, you will please not discuss this matter any further until you and I have had a chance to talk."

"Harrumph," Dad harrumphed. "All right then, Annie. But I'm *not* giving in—to a sixteen-year-old wet-behind-the-ears . . ."

"You will come with me to the Susan B. Anthony Dollar Dance, a week from Friday night, yes, Maximilian?" Justine took both my hands, smiling up at me. Friday night! Due to technical difficulties, your life is being interrupted *again*, Maximilian. Please stand by.

"I haven't heard of the Susan B. Anthony Dollar Dance," I said, sparring for time. We had just finished another widely acclaimed High Noon Show.

"You have not heard of Susan B. Anthony?" She looked shocked at my ignorance.

I had had my consciousness successfully raised. "Of course I've heard of Susan B. Anthony! She was that Victorian lady-libber who got involved in the temperance fight and women's rights. I've even heard of her dollar. In fact, I have some of them cached away. What I haven't heard of is the dance, dum-dum."

"That is because I am just now inviting you, *cher*. The girls invite the boys, yes? It is the plan of the GIG's, the Girls in Government, student government, to make money

to help girl students with troubles. You will come, Maximilian, yes?'' Her smile was dazzling.

"You said on a *Friday* night?'' I probed anxiously.

"Yes, in honor of Susan B. Anthony's birthday, on
February fifteenth.'' She slung her guitar over one shoulder and we started walking to our lockers.

"But February fifteenth is long gone,'' I pointed out.

"The GIG's had to wait until after the basketball games
to get the boys' gym, *cher*. The girls' gym is too small.
Oh, that makes my Tante Celeste very angry! She says the
girls deserve as big a gym as the boys.'' Her eyes flashed.

"But the girls aren't as big as the boys, so it makes
good sense, Cherie.''

She looked at me suspiciously. "You are fooling with
me, Maximilian, you!''

Not as much as I'd like to, I said to myself, smiling. I
put an arm around her, pulling her close. "How come your
Aunt Celeste is letting you slip your leash on a *Friday*
night, Mademoiselle Femme Fatale?'' French One hadn't
been entirely wasted on me; almost, but not entirely.

"My Tante Celeste *wants* me to go—it is my duty to
honor Susan B. Anthony! And she is rooting for those girls
who have troubles, my Tante Celeste, her! *She* is paying,
Maximilian—one dollar for me, and one dollar for you,
one dollar for every cold drink for us! For you it costs
nothing, *cher,* I guarantee!''

Just my job. I was cornered. I'd be canned if I went—
and possibly conned, if I didn't. "You are going, even if
I can't get off that night?''

She said promptly—too promptly, "I will ask Brad
Bedford! He made me late today for the noon show, him.
He wanted to talk to me. He *likes* me—I can tell!''

I could tell, too. Every guy in school probably liked her,

male-fantasized about her, in fact. But Brad Bedford *again,* the Hunk, the captain of the football team? No, my heart thudded. My head took up my cause.

"He's going steady with that cute cheerleader—what's her name? The blonde that looks like Goldie Hawn?"

"Sherry Wilkins. They broke up, *cher,* everybody knows that but you, Maximilian. You live in a closet, with a mirror." She sounded testy.

My heart was winning the fight. "Hey, Cherie—if I lose my job, it's going to make it harder for me to fly down to Houma with you, in April." Bite your tongue, Maximilian Mess-up-your-life Murphy!

She flung her arms around me and I was tempted to suspend all inhibitions, but I couldn't quite ignore the heavy foot traffic around us. Our kiss was short and sweet.

Justine looked up, smiling. "Oh, Maximilian, you are thinking you will come to Houma! Maman is planning on it—and my daddy wants to know, what kind of man is this that I will be marrying? *He* thinks I must marry a good Cajun Catholic, but Maman . . ."

"Marrying?" I interrupted. I could feel the blood draining from my body like soup in a sieve. "Marrying?" I whispered. Then I rallied—I had to. "Who said anything about marriage, Cherie? Not me." I straightened my shoulders. "Hey, we're just kids—only sixteen!"

"We will wait until we are eighteen, you wump," she said patiently.

"Wimp." I said it automatically.

"Yes, wimp. You will be rich and famous by then, Maximilian, so why should we wait any more? We are made for each other, yes?"

I was getting the shakes—those words had come home to roost like hungry buzzards. "Hey, aren't you planning on being the lengendary Belle of the Bayou? Are you giving up your career for a bunch of sniveling kids?'' The thought struck terror into the very marrow of my bones.

"Loretta Lynn had a bunch of sniveling kids, her! *Now* what do you say, Maximilian?'' She stopped, facing me, hands on her hips. Her pink cheeks matched her ski jacket. Her red lips smiled mockingly.

"What is there left to say, Cherie? Actions speak louder than words.'' I kissed her. "As they say.'' Although talk is supposed to be cheap, I felt it could cost me an arm and a leg, and a lifetime, at this point. I said noncommittally, "What band's playing—for the dance?''

"The Winks. Rockabilly and country rock, *cher.*''

"The Winks? Those crazy little sophomore girls? No wonder the GIG's can keep the price down to a dollar!''

She turned adoring eyes on me. "Oh, Maximilian, *cher,* you are *not* a wimp! You are a—a . . .''

"Born loser,'' I supplied, picturing my cash flow tilting towards Houma. I wrapped my arms around her—guitar and all. We didn't care who was looking. Love is blind.

—I know that I, for one, wondered whether your foray into the social and academic milieu of the average high-school student would handicap your progress in music. You know, Burke, I have followed your phenomenal career virtually since your first public performance . . .

—I was six years old. I played the Schubert Sonatina in D Major before the Women's Club of Greater Los Angeles. Were you in the audience, Mr. Aaronson?

—Unfortunately not, but the review in a local paper was brought to my attention. I must say, I have always been a little cautious about proclaiming just any precocious young talent a prodigy. So often a child reaches apogee at age fourteen and stays there while the average talent catches up. But I'm happy to say that I followed up on little Miss Lindstrom and have seen that talent burgeon.

—Thank you. On a scale of one to ten, ten being tops, how would you score my performance tonight?

—Now you've put me on the spot, Burke! You're the celebrity, you know! Frankly, I like to weigh the components of a performance in my mind for an hour or two before committing myself! But didn't the standing ovation tonight—including the shouts and screams from a culturally cultivated audience—tell you something?

—Not really. Today's audiences are too inclined to give any itinerant artist a standing ovation.

—There's a grain of truth in what you say, but in this case the audience was fully justified.

—I went to a chamber music concert in New Orleans last weekend. And would you believe that although the dynamics in the Debussy String Quartet Number Five were all wrong, the audience went wild. I certainly didn't get to my feet.

—You were in New Orleans especially for the con-cert?

—Oh, no. A school friend invited me to Houma dur-ing spring break, so of course I made a point of going to New Orleans first for the concert.

—Was it your first visit to New Orleans?

—Yes, and it may very well be my last. New Orleans has the biggest cockroaches in the world! I had no idea!

—Cockroaches spoiled your visit? They're very com-mon in tropical places, you know.

—But that *big, Mr. Aaronson? Can the camera see this—see my fingers? That long—and* mean-*looking, like tanks! It was* horrible—*devastating! Really worse than the alligators . . .*

★ ★ 11

The day at UCLA wasn't all that great. In the first place, we were having one of our February drizzles—not wet enough to break out the rain gear, but too wet for comfort. Mom decided not to come along after all. She said she was going to pig out on mending instead of chocolates. She had pulled the old equal-opportunity act on Dad and me some time back, in reference to the mending, which was piling up again on her sewing machine. Dad had managed to run the sewing machine needle through one finger and had to go to the emergency room at the hospital. Mom said he did it on purpose. And I had clumsily stitched up a long, crosswise rip in a sheet that inspired some of my best creative thinking. I offered to change the sheets on the beds that week. Around midnight you could hear Dad's roar a block away: "Whoever's responsible for this blasted short-sheeting is in for a cut across the butt! You hear that, Max?"

I was laughing so hard into my blankets I didn't dare answer. By the next morning Dad was mellowing, especially after Mom said, "Maximilian Murphy, you are never to go near my sewing machine again, do you hear?" And Dad had whispered hoarsely, "Good thinking, son," in his conspiratorial we-men-must-stick-together tone.

But I'd rather have been home mending with Mom than trekking Dad's beloved Hills of Westwood. At any moment all creation just had to start crumbling, and it did. We were heading for the student store, against my better judgment.

"No Bear Wear, Dad," I said with foreboding.

"Just window-shopping, Max. By the way . . ." He said it too casually, and I was instantly alert. ". . . you've reconsidered that stupid idea—about quitting school, I presume." It wasn't a great opener.

"No. Sorry, Dad—I know you're disappointed." I braced myself.

"What! I thought I made myself clear!" He stopped and faced me just at the moment the clouds decided to open up. I couldn't see us doing an OK Corral here on this steep asphalt walk all day in a downpour. "Max, you are to graduate with your class and that's final. I positively refuse to permit your dumb, wet-behind-the-ears, stupid, inane, cretin . . ."

"I get the picture," I said hurriedly. "Mind if we head for a dry spot, Dad?"

"What? No, you're going to stand right here and listen to me—all day, if necessary." Dad seemed oblivious to the rain, even as he swiped at the rivulet running from his head down into his eyes.

I started to shiver, even though the rain wasn't all that cold. It was now or never. I leveled. "Look, Dad, you can probably make me go to school, unless I run away, and that's not one of my options. But if you don't sign the form I need to leave school in June, I'm telling you now I'll flunk out of M.V.H.S., and they'll send me to continuation high school—with the rest of the losers." My teeth were chattering.

Dad just looked at me. I was glad he couldn't see my stomach knot up. It was a minute before he said anything. The rain, washing over his face, seemed to take all the color with it, and he stood pale and drained. When he finally answered, his voice was low, conversational. I'd rather have had the verbal buckshot, anytime. "Son, you might want to reconsider that speech. Do you know that what you said is plain *blackmail?*"

My mouth dropped open. I finally managed, "All I said was—"

"I heard you. You're saying you'll save *my* face if I sign some form or other. Well, Max, that's *not* one of my options. But one of *yours* is to be a loser. You're right. Nobody can make you learn. I was hoping you'd want to."

"But, hey, Dad! I'd be graduating with the senior class . . ."

"Corn-green." Dad's voice was filled with disgust. "Wet-behind-the-ears . . ."

"Wet all over," I said, shivering again. "Can we go now, Dad?"

"Come on." Soaked, we hurried along the path towards the student union. "I'm not going to say what I was going to say, out of consideration for your mother," he went on. "So I'll just put it this way. Slow down!" He was puffing when we finally stepped inside the building. "I'm not the best miler on the block, you know. What I was going to say is, you quit Mira Vista and I kick you out. Clear?"

"I thought you promised Mom!"

"I promised we'd talk it over, and we did!"

"And Mom—*agreed?*" I couldn't believe it. Not *my* Mom.

"She agreed that I know more about boys than she does,

since I've been one and she hasn't. I convinced her you can't mollycoddle a wet-behind-the-ears, stupid . . .''

"So okay," I said, reacting finally. "Okay, Dad. No heavy scene! I thought you'd sign the release, but if you won't, that just makes it a little harder. *Not* impossible. Continuation classes are easy, and the schedule is flexible. I can work, and I can make it on my own! I'll prove it! Everybody says I've got talent—"

"Talent!" Dad roared, and a couple of Bear Wear customers turned and stared. Dad lowered his voice. *"Everybody* says! Who's *everybody?* A bunch of high-school kids! Get this straight, Max—real talent's as scarce as hen's teeth.''

"Then how come I personally know so many talented people? There's Justine—and Burke—and . . . and Burke . . .'' I almost added Trinka, but I knew Dad wouldn't buy skating as talent.

"And Burke—and that's all! *That* young girl could probably 'make it on her own,' as you put it—if she *wanted* to. But she obviously loves and values her family too much to cause them the . . .'' He stopped. "Over this way.'' I followed him as he headed into Joe Bruin's Den. "If you're going to be a marathoner, you're going to need a decent outfit.''

I ended up with Bear Wear after all, but I felt like Benedict Arnold. My new yellow shorts had "UCLA" in blue script bordering one leg, and the blue shirt screamed "BRUINS!" in gold block letters across the chest. But Dad was beaming.

"Clothes *can* make the man," he said triumphantly as we tooled home along the freeway. Mom came to the door to meet us, looking anxious. "Annie, get a load of our new college man! Show her, Max!''

Mom grabbed up the new threads and hugged them as I dumped them out of the sack. "Oh, Max!" There were stars in her eyes.

"Hey," I said, apropos of nothing. "Did you know that the guy who invented Murphy's Law is alive and well and living in Belview Beach?"

"Don't tell me *you're* claiming the credit, dear," Mom smiled, carefully folding the shorts and shirt.

"No. It was in *People* magazine. His name is Ed Murphy. And he's right-on."

"Well, if you don't like it—rewrite it, son. One Murphy's as good as another." Dad was in great form.

My boss wasn't ecstatic over my asking for a night off, which I'd expected. What I didn't expect was his, "Well, okay. I was a young bucko once myself. But you're putting me in a bind, Max. I'll have to ask Del to work a back-to-back shift. That means time and a half. You pick up the tab for the extra moola it's going to cost me, and I'll call it square."

"Yes, sir. Thanks, sir." The little VW Bug was still in the picture, but it wasn't exactly filling the frame.

"But don't ask me for a night off again, Max. Unless you've got a doctor's certificate to prove you broke a leg."

I almost wished I had. The dance was a drag from the time I was picked up at eight o'clock until the final debacle. Who should do the picking-up but Brad Bedford, pigskin hero, with his date Gina Morley—in Brad's new, red Honda Accord. It was no secret that a Big Ten college (anonymous) had sent it along after Brad's letter of intent, as a little Valentine's Day present.

"How'd you get roped into this?" I muttered to Justine

in the back seat, under cover of the stereo speakers right behind us. The Blasters were belting out their newest rocker.

"He invited us. You do not have a car and I do not have a car, *cher*. It is nice, hahn? Aunt Celeste is *very* impressed!'' She settled into the glove-soft red upholstery.

"It is *not* nice! I naturally thought Aunt Celeste would be driving us, since you never asked *me* to drive.''

"Why should I ask that, Maximilian? All your daddy lets you drive all by yourself is your bike, hahn?'' She smoothed her ruffled prairie skirt—black, with pink flowers that matched her blouse. She wore little-girl black shoes with straps over pink socks with lace trim.

"Well, you could have asked,'' I said defensively, but she had Dad pegged pretty well, at that. The only time I drove our venerable Ford was when he sat right there beside me. I glanced at the flower she had brought me: "The girls give the flowers this time, Maximilian.'' She had stuck it in a buttonhole in my shirt, a checkered job that I thought might suit the occasion. "How come you got me a pink carnation, Cherie? It makes me look like a fag—some guy will probably ask me to dance.''

"Pink is my favorite color.'' My lollipop smiled complacently.

"I sort of figured that. Hey, it belongs right here, in your hair.'' I tucked it into a silver clip at the side of her head. She didn't have a chance to object; I gathered her in for a long kiss that lasted until we got to school. When we came up for air I saw Bedford's eyes in the rear-view mirror, watching us.

"Keep your eyes on the pike, cowpoke,'' I said loudly,

over the stereo. "You want to buck us out all over the parking lot?"

"You want to take a long walk home, Murphy? Mimes should be seen and not heard!" he guffawed, pulling into a parking space.

"That wasn't very nice, Maximilian," Justine observed as we got out of the car. Gina heard her, and flashed me a friendly smile.

At the door, a militant-looking girl took our tickets. She was wearing khaki pants and shirt and reminded me of the old photos in the fifties' magazines of Ché Guevara, without the beret.

She said briskly, "Hi. Leave your shoes inside the door with the shoe monitor. And no pogo slams. This is a high-class hop." I'd heard of pogo slams—a teen club had finally made the news when it was closed down and boarded up because of them. A punker had killed a guy by using his body as a club, slamming the other punker down onto the dance floor and breaking his neck.

"Right," I said to Mme. Ché. "Yes, ma'am." I doffed an imaginary top hat as I bent low in a sweeping bow. I really got into it and jumped up high, clicking my heels, grinning my widest mime grin. When I came down to earth, there was a round of applause from what turned out to be a line-up behind me. I acknowledged my public, and went into the gym.

"Hey, Justine?" I didn't see her.

"Don't forget your shoes," Gina said, next to me. "This is a sock-hop. The faculty says the floor was nearly ruined last time by the pogo-ing."

I pulled off my shoes. "I wouldn't know how to pogo even if you put a pistol to my feet and yelled, 'Dance!' "

The Winks suddenly struck up. The fast, throbbing rhythm filled the room.

"It's easy," Gina yelled, right next to me. "You just hop up and down!"

"Holy Sacramento!" I peered at my two big toes, sticking out of my socks. "I didn't know I should've worn designer socks!" Reluctantly, I handed my shoes over to the shoe monitor, who slipped them into a bag and gave me the claim check.

The music boomed relentlessly. I glanced at the bandstand at the end of the room. How could five little sophomore girls manage to deafen a whole high-school population? The lead singer, a tiny blonde in a rhinestone cowboy outfit, was a female Jerry Lee Lewis by the time her voice shot out of the amps that were twice her size.

I caught Gina's eye and mimed, "Where's Justine?", indicating the swirl of the prairie skirt, and the waist-length hair.

She nodded, and shouted into my ear. It wasn't all that hard, since she was a good five feet eleven, one of those thin model-types with cheekbones and shoulder-length hair, despite which everyone knew Gina Morley was going to be a lawyer. She was already chief justice on the student court. "Dancing with Brad! I said, dancing with Brad! See?"

I looked where she pointed, out into the stomping melee, and picked out Justine and Brad facing each other, moving their feet, and holding hands. Holding hands! It was instant fury. Technically, according to Dad, the first and the last dances were to be with a guy's own girl, and at intermission he was to buy her a Kola King. I was surprised Dad didn't insist on a "dance card," to be filled out as quickly as possible, like in the old romance magazines. "Miss Justine, ma'am, may I have the first, the last, and all the dances in between, please?"

I put my hands over my ears. If loud is good, the Winks had it made. Gina smiled and pulled some cotton out of a small handbag. She stuffed two wads in her ears, and offered some to me. I did the same.

"All the musicians wear earplugs," she shouted into my swaddled ear. "Really! Otherwise they couldn't stand it!"

"Dance?" I mouthed courageously. She nodded, and we threaded our way to a clear spot on the floor, where we improvised until the end of the set. At least at a sock-hop no three-inch spike could shatter my instep, or a heavy heel destroy a toe or two. I'd heard of it happening.

We were padding back towards the benches when I saw them—Justine and Bedford. They thought they were hidden behind a six-foot cardboard replica of a Susan B. Anthony dollar. Brad had pinned Justine's arms and was about to kiss her when I moved in like Grant taking Richmond, as they say.

"Now just hold it, Hunk . . ." I grabbed Justine, and glared at him.

"You—Brad!" Justine screamed, suddenly free. She let go with a haymaker that reverberated through the gym.

"That's my kind of woman!" the Hunk howled, while he rubbed his cheek. She slapped him again, on the other cheek, and he grabbed her hands. "You dynamite little Cajun broad! Come here! I'm gonna show you . . ."

"Here come the fuzz," Gina said. "And I hope they throw the book at you—which is what *I'll* do if you come before the bench, lover-boy."

We were surrounded by faculty watchdogs.

"See here—no rough stuff! What's this all about?" It was the chem teacher.

"Just a little misunderstanding," the Hunk said smoothly, but Mr. Neff didn't buy it.

"You, young lady—have you been drinking?" He took Justine by the elbow.

"I do *not* drink! For shame for you to ask! For shame!" She looked ready to hit him too, and he backed off.

"All right," another teacher insisted. "Are drugs involved? Come on, let's clear this up!"

"No drugs, sir, nothing but a—fiesty young lady, sir." Brad smiled genially. "You have my word, Doctor Neff."

Mr. Neff wasn't exactly a Ph.D., but he smiled, obviously pleased. "Well, we can't have fiesty young ladies on the loose at a school function, Bradley. So shape up or ship out, folks."

They left, and I took Justine's arm and propelled her back towards the benches. "Come on, feisty young dumdum."

She saw the Snow Cone before I did. "Maximilian, look who is here!"

I did a double take. Burke Lindstrom sat straight and unsmiling—beside her *father*. Mom Lindstrom wasn't there, but she had plainly blown the coed look again. Burke stood out like spun sugar at a chili cook-off in that long, lacy white dress that was straight out of the Junior Cotillion.

"Hey, Burke," I said in my normal voice, since the Winks were still, thankfully, asleep, "what are you doing at a rockabilly hop, anyway?" I stared at her delicately stockinged feet—victims of the shoe monitor. Then I remembered the common courtesies, as Mom says, and introduced Justine to Burke's dad.

Justine gasped. "You brought your *father* to the Susan

B. Anthony Dollar Dance, Burke? But that is—that is, well, I guess that is—all right,'' she ended lamely.

Mr. Lindstrom laughed. "I hope it's all right. I'm here. But I *do* feel a bit undressed, without my shoes."

Burke didn't smile. "Father and I simply came to see a public-high-school dance," she said. "Of course *I* don't intend to dance—I'm sure I couldn't manage, anyway. Not unless there's a Viennese waltz. Father and I adore dancing the Viennese waltz."

"Ha," I said. "Don't count on it. The Winks probably never heard of Strauss, except for Levi Strauss."

"Princess, why don't you go out on the floor with Maximilian? Everybody's dancing by themselves—doing their own thing you'd say." He laughed. "You came to Mira Vista to share the realm of your peers—and this is it, right, Maximilian?"

"Well, er . . ." I started to say.

"I don't know—I'm dressed all wrong." Burke looked worried. "I feel so—so—conspicuous!"

I silently agreed with her, but her father laughed heartily. "Oh, for heaven's sake, Princess! You look a thousand times prettier than any girl here, excluding present company, of course." He nodded gallantly towards Justine, who smiled modestly, totally out of character.

The Winks hit the air with a low drum-roll.

"Well, it *isn't* touch-dancing. If you think I should, Father . . ." Burke stood up, fluffing out her skirt. I was trapped.

"Of course I think you should, Princess! Why else are we here? Sit down and keep me company, Justine, while those two be-bop." It was out of my hands. I still hadn't asked her.

The Winks shifted gears and went high-decibel as Burke and I picked our way through the pogo-ing. Heads turned in our direction, but Burke didn't notice; she was watching the flying feet around us. We found our spot, and she began moving cautiously up and down with the beat. I was starting to get into it, jumping as though I was stomping out an invasion of grasshoppers, when I noticed she was starting to panic. You could tell by her animal eyes. Suddenly she stopped her weird nondancing and clapped her hands over her ears.

I was about to mime, "Want to leave?" when a pink and black blur caught my eye. I turned and saw Justine in the clutches of Bedford. He had pinned her arms behind her and was bending over her, doing cheek-to-cheek to rockabilly. Her eyes flagged me down. I promptly forgot Burke and bulldozed over to them, giving the Hunk a mean shove. He looked up, surprised, but he didn't come unglued from Justine, so I aimed a sharp jab at his jaw. It missed and landed on his shoulder, but at least it split them apart.

Justine grabbed my arm and started hauling us through the crowd. Burke came up from behind and latched on to Justine. I didn't know Brad was following until I saw him shove Burke out of the way with both hands as he moved in next to Justine, just at the moment the music stopped.

"You touched me! You touched me!" Burke's shriek rang out over the high-volume chatter that bounced around the room.

Of course all eight faculty chaperones came on like SWAT. I would have even felt sorry for Brad if he hadn't been at the top of my hit list. He tried to melt away in the crowd, but Mr. Neff grabbed him.

"What *is* going on, Bradley? Now we just can't have

any more of . . .'' The Winks hit the percussions, and all I saw were mouths moving soundlessly, then Mr. Neff was escorting Brad off the dance floor.

Burke had disappeared, and when Justine and I got back to the benches, Mr. Lindstrom had too. But Gina materialized, on the arm of one of the Student Court judges a foot shorter than she was. Brad grabbed Gina's and Justine's elbows and yanked both of them towards the shoe monitor's counter. Surprised, I snaked through the crowd, reaching for Justine—but somebody always managed to pogo between us.

"Maximilian, Maximilian!" I could barely hear Justine's shriek.

I yelled, "Hey, Bedford—stop! *We're* not going home with you! Stop!" He probably couldn't hear me, and he probably didn't want to. He was at the counter, and I could see him clutching the claim checks. I almost caught him as he headed for the exit, juggling three pairs of shoes and the two girls. He pushed Justine out the door ahead of him. Gina followed, snatching at her shoes under his arm. I saw her get one of them and give him a crack over the head with it. Vigilante justice. He winced—this time the hero wasn't wearing a helmet.

"That's for breach of contract, you melonhead!" she projected, and he reached back and grabbed her arm, hustling her out the door.

"C'mon, Gina! I'm going to make it up to you—to both . . ." was all I heard as the words hit the night.

I forgot about my own shoes and tore out after them. Mme. Ché stopped me, stepping in front of me.

"Say, friend, how come you're running around with naked toes? Forget your shoes?" She grinned at me.

"Look out, lady!" I yelled. "I'm coming through!"

"Nobody leaves without their shoes somewhere on them." She stood her ground. "The GIG's refuse to be held liable for lost leather, sonny. Go get 'em." She glared at me.

I hated to do it to a genuine lady guerrilla, but I suddenly stomped on her toes in my tattered socks. She yelled, "Hey!" and moved just enough for me to rush by her. Ahead of me, I saw the three of them reach the car. Justine was gasping breathlessly, "Oh, help! Let me go, you, Brad!" Gina appeared to be arguing, but Brad's laughs were drowning her out.

I was closing in—I don't do the mile in 4:20 for nothing. Brad flung open the rear door of the car and threw something in, shouting, "Go get 'em, Cinderella! Where'll it be, girls—supper and dancing at the Spindrift on the pier?"

I was almost within grabbing distance when the Hunk picked up Justine and tossed her into the back seat. Gina was already in the front seat; he dashed around the front of the car and jumped in beside her. I reached the Accord and wrenched the handle of the rear door. Justine was frantically pulling at the lock post and yelling, "Maximilian! Oh, help me!" The door didn't budge—probably electrically locked.

"Watch it, Dumbo!" Bedford shouted at me. The car leaped into gear and made a fast U-turn. I jumped back as it raced up beside me. "Nice night for a hike home, Bonzo!"

Gina said loudly, "Let her out, Brad! This isn't funny! Kidnapping's a felony! The law states . . ." Her voice cut out as the Accord burned rubber.

I stood—abandoned and bewildered—in the middle of a dark parking lot. But only for a minute. I turned as I heard a car coming towards me, and started to sprint in case it was Bedford on a chicken run. It wasn't. It was the long, white boat-tail job.

"Need a ride, Maximilian?" Mr. Lindstrom leaned from the window. "I saw what happened."

"Yes, sir, I guess I do—need a hitch. But first I need my shoes . . ." I briefly explained my shoeless state.

"We'll wait, Maximilian," Burke said from the front seat beside her father. "Go back in and get your shoes."

"I can't. I'll be shot down by that lady guerrilla at the door."

Mr. Lindstrom said promptly, "I'll go get them for you. After I park." He swung the car into the spot Brad had left, and got out. "There are some advantages to getting older—not many, but pulling rank is one of them. Where's your claim check?" He left for the gym. I stood beside the car.

"Don't worry, Maximilian," Burke said serenely. "That boy won't hurt Justine. He has too much at stake, he can't afford a scandal. And he has Gina with him, too. Everything will be all right."

"I'm glad you think so!" I exploded. "If you hadn't wanted to collect just one more *peer-group experience* everything *would* have been all right! Why don't you stay out of places where you *know* you're going to get *touched?*"

"Oh, Maximilian—it was a chance to escape from Angelica! And I thought there might be—Viennese waltzes! I *love* Viennese waltzing!"

I laughed scornfully. "At a *rockabilly* dance?" I saw her swipe at her eyes. "Why did you want to escape from your mother? Did *she* want to come too?" Unbelievable.

"She doesn't leave me alone for a second, anymore—

that is, outside her working hours, and she even manages to arrange *those* around *my* activities. She insistes on going with me to my music coach's studio, in Father's place. She drives me to the drugstore when all I want is a little exercise and maybe a new lipstick. She even goes to chamber music concerts with me, and she *hates* chamber music! Oh, it's terrible! Father and I are used to doing everything together!''

In the back of my mind I heard the frantic voice, ''Darling, I'll *never* leave you alone again . . .'' I gulped, and hoped I sounded—well, bland. ''Uh, she's not here with you tonight. So she isn't with you *all* the time.''

''Oh, Father and I had to scheme to get away from her tonight, Maximilian! We lied! We told her this was a father-daughter dance! That's why I'm dressed this way—I had a feeling it might not be right!''

I had to laugh inside. Mom Lindstrom was gullible. Father-Daughter Night had practically died with the dinosaurs.

''I don't know what I'm going to do! My mother is driving me crazy!'' She looked distraught, and I was glad her father reappeared just then. He handed me my shoes.

''You might want to put them on now,'' he said, ''if you're going to drive.''

It took me by surprise. He was a nice guy. ''Drive?'' But this just wasn't cloud-nine time. ''Thanks, sir. But not this time—not now.''

I got into the back seat, holding my shoes. We drove home in silence.

"My Tante Celeste was very angry with you, Maximilian. She says you should have called her, you," Justine said Saturday morning. There were dark circles under her eyes.

"And said *what,* Cherie? 'Hey, Aunt Celeste, I've lost Justine!' What good would *that* do?" I looked at her closely. "By the way, what *did* you do—stay out all night? You look terrible."

"Ha! You look terrible too, you, but do I say so, Maximilian? No! Look at you, with your crazy hair sticking out like a straw man!" She broke into fake laughter.

I ignored it. "So, get on with it—what happened last night? I ought to kick the socks off that Bedford clown— he kidnapped you! We could make trouble for him!"

"Oh, no need for trouble, *cher,*" she said airily. "We had a very nice time. We went to the Spindrift on the pier. Gina and I took turns dancing with Brad, us, and you should see what a supper we had! Maximilian, do you know what lobster thermidor *costs?*"

"Don't tell me," I snapped. "In fact, don't tell me any more at all—except, when did you get in? I worried all night about you, Miss Swinger!"

"Yes, you do look bad, Maximilian. You have ugly

black circles. I got home at four o'clock. Oh, Tante Celeste was *so* angry, all the time she was crying!''

"Did he kiss you—*did* he?'' Did I really want to know? She looked offended. "Of *course* he kissed me!''

"How come *of course?*'' I shouted. "You *let* him, didn't you—you—Jezebel!''

"Oh—*she* was a wicked woman! For shame, Maximilian—calling me—that name!'' She looked infuriated.

"Did you *let* him?'' I grabbed her by the shoulders. "Or did he—as they say—take *advantage* of you?'' I gave her a sharp shake, and her hair flew out, the soft, silky strands brushing my chin. Once again my stern resolve dissolved. I kissed her.

She looked up. "Oh, Maximilian—he does not kiss like you!'' I felt compelled to prove my superiority again.

We were standing in our dark garage, the only private place on the Murphy rancho. We had to share our space with the collectible Ford, my bike, garden equipment, and a large shelf loaded with everything from camping gear to ancient trunks.

"I had to sneak out, to tell you, Maximilian. I am grounded. My Tante Celeste is still asleep—I think, her. And so I cannot go with you, on the bike ride today. Maybe never!''

"What! The Hunk's the one who should be grounded! Your Aunt Celeste is depriving *me* of my R and R! It's unfair!'' It was also dirty tricks.

"R and R, Maximilian?''

"Recreation and rehabilitation, which I badly need, Cherie! Why is your Aunt Celeste doing this to me?'' My eyes wandered over her T-shirt, ogling a stamped-on message.

"She is doing it to *me,* Maximilian, because I scared

her.'' Our eyes locked. My heart began thumping double time.

"Why didn't you phone her from the Spindrift? What's your T say, anyway?'' *Mentally,* my fingers were outlining the letters.

"Louisiana Sugar—It's the Sweetest. It's an ad, Maximilian. Because she would have come there to the Spindrift and hit Brad and lectured him on male chauvinist hog, and she would have grabbed me and taken me home! It would have been very—embarrassing, yes?''

"Very,'' I murmured, gathering her in. During our long embrace I eased her T-shirt out of her jeans.

"No feelies!'' she roared, just as the garage door swung open. We were caught in the full glare of Saturday-morning sunshine.

Dad said blandly, "Oh, there you are. Justine, your aunt called. She wants you home—pronto.''

Justine snatched at her T, stuffing it into her jeans. "Oh! She is awake! Oh, oh!'' She got on her aunt's silver ten-speed, just outside the door. "Maximilian, it is soon Houma! You do not forget . . .'' She pedaled frantically off.

I said lamely, "We were about to get my bike and . . .''

"You were about to contribute to the delinquency of a minor,'' Dad snorted.

"But, hey, Dad—I'm a minor myself! That doesn't wash!''

"You were *messing around,*'' he said shortly. He glared at me—then he broke up. "Nothing's changed!'' he gasped. He glanced at the storage shelf, then did a double take. "Say—there's Granddad's old steamer trunk! I haven't looked in there yet. Help me get it down.''

We easily lifted the old domed-top trunk down and un-buckled the disintegrating leather straps. Dad opened the lid. "How about that—empty, except for—how about that!" He picked up a lethal-looking strap. "Granddad's old razor strop!" He ran his fingers over it, then looked at me, thoughtfully. "Say, son—you've been thinking about this quitting school business, haven't you—construc-tively?" He tested the leather, stretching it.

I thought for a long minute. "Nothing's changed."

Justine was still grounded the Saturday of the Kola King Marathon. I was hoping for a record-breaking kiss when I crossed the finish line, but she said, "I cannot be there, Maximilian. My Tante Celeste says she will send me back to Houma forever if I break any more rules, me. Oh, I am very careful, Maximilian, you can be sure. Houma is a nice place to *visit* . . ."

"Roberto Rodriguez, running for the Mira Vista Track Club, number one forty-two," the official at the registra-tion table said, checking his list. He handed the Rabbit a large number on stiff paper. "Maximilian Murphy. Inde-pendent. Number one forty-three. Pin your numbers on the *front* of your shirts. Next, please . . ."

Sign-up was in the hallway of Hilltop High School. The race would start on the closed-off street out in front, and end at the community park twenty six miles, three-hundred eighty-five yards later.

"I heard there are three thousand sign-ups," the Rabbit said as we worked our way through the jam-packed hall-way and out the back doors. It was good to shake the smell of running shoes and sweat.

"And you can bet another thousand didn't preregister and are doing it now, and another five hundred will just jump in for the heck of it," I said.

We picked out Dad in his royal blue parka—he was easy to spot, one of the few in the crowd *not* milling around. He had hauled out of bed at five-thirty. We had picked up the Rabbit at Cousin Mario's, which turned out to be in nearby Playa de Reynosa, and we'd gotten here at the top of the hill in Cuesta Verde, fifteen miles away, at six-thirty. The race would start in an hour.

"Hey, boys!" Dad called. "You want to get warm in the car? Mom sent hot chocolate!" It was a tempting offer. The sky had gradually gone from moonless black to dawn's misty gray. It was cold—the best marathon weather, if it would only hold.

The Rabbit and I were both wearing heavy fleece-lined sweats. His were dark blue, mine gray. Underneath I had secretly put on my lucky old red nylon shorts and the gold T from my only previous official marathon try: "Echo Bay Finisher," it lied. I had had to drop out after fifteen miles, barfing from too much hot chocolate on top of too much French toast. This time I'd loaded up on my carbos the night before. There were plenty of carbohydrates in three soupbowls of spaghetti. This morning was strictly liquid diet.

"Let's save the chocolate until after the race," I said tactfully. Mom had gotten up with Dad and me and made the chocolate this morning, then had gone back to bed. She had to work today. "But we'd better down a little ERG right now, before it gets any later."

"I know I *have* to drink," the Rabbit said. "Even though I do not *like* that stuff before a race."

We were at the car and Dad opened the trunk.

"At least you run fast enough to sweat it out, Rabbit," I said. "You never have to p . . ."

"And there's all that ERG at the aid stations," the Rabbit went on impassively. I poured the drinks from the thermos into paper cups, and handed one to the Rabbit.

"ERG," Dad said. "Let's see, that stands for . . ."

"Electrolytic replacement with glucose. It used to be called Gookinaid," I said. "Invented by Mr. Gookin."

"You will sweat it out this time, Mox." The Rabbit gulped his cupful. "You run very fast now, since you stop wastin' time with women."

"I *like* wasting time with women," I muttered, and the Rabbit laughed. I drained my cup.

"You will like comin' in win, place, or show, Mox."

"No way." And I wasn't being modest. This race attracted some of the best road-runners in the field, but I'd bet a bundle the Rabbit would finish in the money, as they say.

"You be sure you drink plenty, and pour plenty of water on your head, Mox," the Rabbit advised. "You dry out, you've had it, Mox."

"Right." I closed the container. "I just hope I don't have to p . . ."

"Quit thinking about it," Dad said. "You always have to if you think about it."

"Let's warm up," the Rabbit said. "Couple, three miles aroun' the trock. Nice and easy."

"If I don't see you before—see you at the finish line." Dad locked the trunk. "Wish I could drive along with you, like last time, when we set up our free-drinks and first-aid concession every five miles, off the tailgate. That was pretty interesting."

"That was a small-time race, Dad. Most of the big ones now—they don't allow cars on the road at all, except the pickup van for the deadwood. They don't even like bicycles. Too many runners."

"Well, I'm going to try to drive to that overlook at about the halfway point, see if I can spot you two down below," Dad said. "Good luck!"

The Rabbit and I jogged an easy mile around the track with a few thousand other joggers, then went into the infield for leg stretches and body bends. "Two miles more around the trock, Mox," the Rabbit urged, finishing with jumping jacks.

"That will make twenty-nine miles, three hundred eighty-five yards for us today! Let's not overdo it, Rabbit!"

The Rabbit laughed and took off at a fast pace. I followed at an easy lope. After all, there was no Tarahumara blood in *my* veins. I wanted to be warmed up, not worn out, when the starter's gun went off.

The Rabbit could have been seeded, but he said he didn't care about *that* stuff, he would rather start with me—right in the middle of the pack. He could, he said matter-of-factly, pick off those guys up front any time he wanted to, anyway. "Those guys" were the cream of the country, but so was the Rabbit. Friendship was *worth* the nine bucks it cost me!

We couldn't do a thing to begin with, but go with the flow, as they say. Four thousand runners create a current like a riptide, and all you want to do is keep your head above water until you break away from the pack.

So we were about three miles into the race before I spotted my nemesis—the unmistakable redhead, Burke Lindstrom. On her white bike, in her white jeans and windbreaker. And—double-trouble—her *mom* was biking right behind her! "Oh, no!" I groaned. They were riding on the far side of the road, so busy avoiding runners that they didn't see me glance their way.

I sprinted up to the Rabbit's side. "Rabbit, it's *them*— Burke, and her mom, I think! I can't believe it! How'd they get permission, anyway? Now what do we do?"

"Keep runnin', Mox. Maybe they will get los'. You see now, Mox—you *got* to stay away from women, like me." He chugged cheerfully along, his short dark legs, made up entirely of knotted muscles, striking out strong and effortlessly. He was wearing the M.V.H.S. colors, green cotton gym shorts and a white message T the guys in cross-country had given him when he won the state trophy for them: "I'm #1." It was, he said, his lucky T, and with it he became invincible (as if he weren't, already!). "Now, Mox!" He nodded at me, and we jumped ahead, pouring it on just long enough to catch the front-runners, but not passing them. We had our strategy: we'd keep contact with the leaders until about mile twenty-four, when we'd make our big move out front.

I heard "Hi, Maximilian!" coming from across the road. They had followed us—and unluckily their chances of "getting lost" were pretty remote, now that we'd left the pack. I didn't look at either of them, and I didn't answer Burke.

"Jus' ignore them, Mox," was the Rabbit's stoic advice, "an' they will go away." He didn't know much about women.

Suddenly Burke's bike was beside me. "I said, hi, Maximilian!" When I charged steadily ahead, following the Rabbit's advice, she wasn't at all discouraged. "Angelica and I are carrying squeeze bottles full of ERG, for you and Roberto." I stared stonily at the road, keeping up with the Rabbit. "Just signal when you're ready!"

"Go away, Burke!" I exploded. "I'm busy!"

"We're here to help," she said with determination, staying with me. At least her mom had the good sense to keep on the far side of the road. I expected the Snow Cone to swerve at any second and send me reeling, out of the race for good. "We found out all about marathons at the Phidippidean Experience." The PE was the "in" runners' shop downtown. I had to begrudgingly hand it to the Snow Cone, descending like Marceau's angel from her rarified atmosphere into the earthy milieu of shinsplints, sweat, and shattered dreams.

"The PE should have told you about the stations!" In other words, Snow Cone, you can stuff your squeeze bottles.

"They did, but I thought, what if you and Roberto need a drink *between* those stands!"

"Go back, Burke, just go back! You aren't supposed to be here on the road. You're illegal." I hated talking when I was into my stride. Running was a wedding of mind and body, with mind in charge of pacing and rhythm and body in charge of breathing and strength. Talking blows the timing like a ripe tomato at a mime show.

Now Mom Lindstrom biked into the act. "Oh, it's all right, Maximilian. Burke's father spoke to the authorities, and we have official permission." He must've pulled a *lot* of rank—nothing on wheels but the official cars was supposed to be on the course from sundown last night until the end of the race today. "But I must say," she went on sharply, "I think this idea of Burke's is perfectly ridiculous."

"Well, Angelica, you didn't need to come, you know!"

Burke shouted. "I planned to do this all by myself! I wish you'd just leave me alone!"

I said silently, And I just wish you'd leave *me* alone, Burke Lindstrom! You're traumatizing my tranquillity! I snapped out loud, "Watch where you're going! Get over on the other side of the road!" She had started to weave.

"Do you want a squeeze-bottle yet?" she called, when they had both crossed the road.

"Do you want a squeeze bottle yet, babykins?" some nerd behind me mimicked in falsetto, laughing. I hoped he'd trip over his big mouth.

"Yeah, baby, nursie is ready and willing!" A minipack of jackals behind me joined in a chorus of happy yelps. I felt my ears flash fire, and the heat covered my whole face. I churned straight ahead.

"Don' worry, Mox," the Rabbit said easily. "You will be crossin' the finish line before the von brings those guys in."

The first aid-station was at mile eight. I was still happy with my one cup of ERG, but I wasn't anxious for any more. The Rabbit grabbed a paper cup from the table labeled ERG and ordered, "You drink too, Mox! Every time you get a chance!" He drank and tossed the cup aside.

I imagined Burke's eyes on me. I picked up a paper cup as I whipped by the stand marked WATER, and poured the contents over my head. No matter how cold the air is, you sweat like a stevedore when you're running, and you lose most of the sweat through your head. I'd have to keep a cool, *wet* head.

At about mile nine, Burke shouted from across the road, "Now, Maximilian?"

"Now, man! Bikers do it in the dirt!" came a voice

behind me, followed by a burst of laughter. My face got hotter—and, I was sure, redder.

A girl's voice said witheringly, "Knock it off, creeps!"

"A girl!" I said to the Rabbit. "A *girl* is catching us! We better pour it on, Rabbit!"

"Don' worry, Mox. A girl movin' up this fos', she will fade jus' as fos', you will see." He was unflappable.

We'd been running on a fairly level road overlooking the ocean, after a good downhill start from Hilltop High School. Now the course was starting to climb, a relentless, constant grade. You could feel it in your lungs and leg muscles. Despite my sand hill workouts, I knew when I was fighting gravity—the quadriceps protested, and breathing came a little harder.

"Burke, not so fast! I can't keep up!" It was a shout from Mom Lindstrom, and I grinned. There was something to be said for gravity, after all. With luck, they'd both soon bite the dust.

"Go sit under a tree then, Angelica! Father and I will pick you up later! *I* am going on!" I glanced at Burke. She was pedaling briskly, not even in lowest gear. She was stronger than she looked, but she'd already proved that at her Sunday soirée, as they say. I decided that strong women were *not* for me.

The Rabbit and I maintained contact with the front-runners, staying maybe thirty yards behind them. An official with a stopwatch called out from the middle of the road, "Mile thirteen! Sixty-five twenty-one, sixty-five twenty-two, sixty-five . . ." We were just over an hour into the race. The time wasn't bad, but there were more hills ahead. Thirteen miles—about halfway. I thought of Dad, and looked up to the top of the bluff to see if he'd made it to the overlook. I saw the bright blue parka—he was there, leaning over the railing, and waving.

"Hang in there, *traitor!*" His shout floated down to us, as we ran by just below. I gave the thumbs-up signal, grinning. It had just come to me that I was inadvertently wearing the detested colors of UCLA's cross-town rival—cardinal and gold. If I blew the race, Dad would have the last laugh!

At the next aid-station, the Rabbit grabbed two paper cups. He gulped the ERG and dumped the water over his head. The sun was coming on strong—it felt hotter than it should have before nine A.M. I grabbed a cup of water, spilling it over my head.

"You be sorry, Mox! How long since you drink?"

"I'm still going on my early ERG!"

Burke rode up to me, holding out a squeeze bottle. "Here, Maximilian—drink this!"

She infuriated me. Who asked for a nursemaid? I waved her aside. "Get away, Burke!" She was messing up my pacing. Come on, body, you've got to dance with mind! The harder I tried, the more my breathing objected—coming short and hard instead of long and easy, to match my stride. She was getting to me. I couldn't let her.

"You take thot squeeze bottle from thot girl now, Mox! You hear? Your face is red! You drink now, for sure!" The Rabbit was just ahead of me. When he turned to look at me, I could see he was scowling. I knew it was getting harder for him to hold back for me—he could smell the barn.

"No! Not yet! I'll take a cup at the next station!" I wouldn't give in to her.

"You promise, Mox? I'm watchin' you!"

I nodded. "You go on ahead, Rabbit! I'm right behind you! Go home, Rabbit!"

"Pretty soon, Mox! We both go home! Come on!" I caught up with him, but it wasn't as easy as it should have been. We were running along a residential street. The curbs were lined with people cheering us on and holding garden hoses in the air, so that the water arched into the road. You could run through the spray or miss it. I was burning up, so I made sure I ran through it. The Rabbit did too, catching every hose on the street.

I kept my word regarding ERG. At mile eighteen I grabbed two cupfuls and gulped both of them. We'd run out of friendly garden hoses, and were skirting the golf course. The day shouldn't be all this hot—the sun was pale and misty-looking in the eastern sky.

The Rabbit glanced at me. "You okay, Mox? You look hot."

"I am," I said.

He motioned to Burke. "Here, girl! You give him thot squeeze bottle, okay?" She came over on her bike and held out the bottle.

"Mox, you squirt that stuff on your head, you hear?" the Rabbit ordered, grabbing the bottle and poking it at me.

"I don't need a nursemaid—two nursemaids!" I wouldn't take it.

He pulled the stopper and dumped the bottle's contents over my head. It was ERG—sticky ERG! "You dummy, Mox! You goin' to blow firs' place!"

"Well," I said grimly, swiping at the rivulets pouring down my face, "don't *you* blow it. Thanks—Rabbit! Go home!" He seemed uncertain. I scowled and jabbed my finger in the direction of the finish, and he nodded and took off—a Porsche turbo on the straight.

"You can do it too, Maximilian! Go, Maximilian!" Burke shouted, right beside me.

"Go, boy! Fetch, boy! Good boy!" The jibes came from right behind me. I turned, startled, and saw the minipack on my heels. I shifted gears and highballed into mile twenty.

At mile twenty-two I decided I didn't want to break stride for a drink. I had never run stronger. Some of the front-runners had dropped back and I easily passed them. A few others were lying in the weeds beside the road, casualties of "the wall." I glanced at my watch—nine-fifteen. I wanted to cross home base by nine-forty-five. Clearly, I'd have to be hit by a miracle. Hey, miracle—here I come! I poured it on, ignoring a creeping fatigue.

It must have been mile twenty-four when, breathing too hard, I slowly shuffled to a stop and sank down at the side of the road—like the other losers. I closed my eyes—panting, exhausted, but not too out of it to be plenty mad. Mile twenty-four—where the Rabbit and I were going to break for the roses! What had gone wrong? My head whirled—it was the champagne trip in spades. I didn't even try to get up.

A warmish wave washed over my head. Startled, I ran a hand over my eyes and opened them. I saw Burke bending over me, an uncorked squeeze bottle in her hand.

"You dumbhead," I gasped. "Go away! Get away from me!" I was drowning in ERG and impotent fury.

"Maximilian! Are you all right?" She was kneeling beside me. Streams of runners were flowing by us—even girls and little kids—one didn't look more than ten years old; he was really leaning into it. They were all headed home. Nobody even glanced at me—the fallen.

"Sure. I'm just *great*—thanks to you!" It was clear now what had happened: I'd let her get to me. Twenty-four miles of needling did it. I got dehydrated to spite her. I glared at her, hating that frozen-yogurt face, those blueberry eyes. It was her fault.

My glare must not have been as fierce as it felt. She said, "Yes. I'm glad I was here to help. It's too bad you couldn't go on, Maximilian. You had passed almost everybody."

"I wish I'd passed *you!* Why couldn't you leave me alone? I was busting my butt—this was the most important race of my life—and *you* made me blow it!" Rage was strengthening. I propped myself up on my elbows.

"Maximilian! Are you trying to blame your failure on *me?* Why, that's—outrageous! You can just stay here by yourself until the van picks you up." She stood up. I was pleased to see grass stains all over her white jeans. "Goodbye."

I sat up, leaning back on my hands for support. "Wait a minute—let me get something straight. Did you by any chance—pull this guardian-angel act just to *experience* a marathon—like that rockabilly romp? Is this one of your *real*-world gigs?" My voice was a hoarse whisper.

She looked down at me, unsmiling. "Partly." She couldn't lie if she had to.

"So you are using me *again*—for another little adventure?" I was ticked, and doubly ticked that I didn't sound as enraged as I felt.

"That's not entirely true, Maximilian. I also wanted to repay you, a little bit, for all the nice things you've done for me. Just last Thursday you got that foolish Mrs. Hodges to stop calling me 'he' and 'him' . . .''

"You could've just said thank you!" I crackled, struggling to my feet so that I could look down on *her*. "Why do you have to be an albatross around my neck?" I swayed a little.

She stepped back, surprised, and her face turned red. "I don't have to listen to . . ." She turned, in sudden fury, and started to run—but as luck would have it, my foot was in the way. She fell. Flat, in the weeds.

I reached for her, automatically, and pulled her to her feet. I have never gone in for deliberately decking a girl.

She screamed, like the wild peacocks you hear in these hills. She screamed and screamed, "You *touched* me!"

She climbed onto her bike and pedaled off, weaving crazily, just as the van cautiously crept over the hill. I started walking. I refused to be carted off like a side of beef. I'd cross the finish line—on my feet.

★ ★ *13*

The Rabbit and I met at the track Monday morning, but not to work out—to hold a post-mortem.

"You were on the five o'clock and eleven o'clock news Saturday," I said, trying to sound matter-of-fact. "You were in the *Daily Dune* Saturday night. And the *Times* gave you a picture and a good story yesterday morning. Here, I brought you the clippings." I took an envelope from my pocket and handed it to him.

"Thanks, Mox. Mama will want to keep them. They will make her feel good when she is not feeling so good, like today."

"You were great—stupendous, Rabbit! You're a shoo-in for the Olympics, now." My voice dripped with envy as thick as molasses.

The Rabbit looked somber. "I am a shoo-in for getting kicked out of the U.S., Mox. The INS has big eyes. Those guys see TV and the sports page too. I should not have done it."

"Done what? You mean you shouldn't have *won* the marathon?"

"That's what I mean, Mox. I was stupid to win." He unfolded the big *Times* clipping without enthusiasm. The headline screamed, RODRIGUEZ COPS KOLA KING

CROWN. "Look at that! Those INS guys can spot me easy now, Mox!"

"You're paranoid, Rabbit. Why do you think they're out to get *you,* especially?"

"They're out to get *someone,* Mox, and me, now I'm goin' to be easy to find!"

"You aren't going to hide out any more?"

"Who can hide a wart on the nose, Mox? Anyway, the steaks at the barbecue after the race were good. I ate two! Real porterhouse steaks, Mox!"

Dad and I had hung around on the fringes of the festivities, smelling the steaks and waiting for the Rabbit, the celebrity of the day. He'd run the distance in two-eight and thirty seconds, setting a new course record.

"They didn't offer a steak to the dropouts," I said bitterly.

"Just to the top fifty finishers, Mox. But *you* can eat steak any time."

"Maybe." I thought about it. "And next time we have it—*you're* invited. Your mom, too." I wasn't bitter any more.

I stayed away from Burke for the rest of the week. But every time I caught a glimpse of her, her weird purple eyes were watching me. She looked sad, and right now I was glad. She deserved to be miserable.

"Wait a minute, Maximilian Murphy. You've been avoiding me," she said, somewhat perceptively, as I got ready to do my amen-sprint at the end of history class on Friday. All I wanted was to get home, sprawl out on my bed, and finish reading Agna Enters on Mime. I wanted to forget fame and the marathon, and concentrate on fortune and my career.

"How'd you guess?" I snapped. Who needed her?

"Are you still blaming me because you collapsed at that marathon?"

"Of course I am!" I exploded, turning and walking away.

"Maximilian—wait!" She caught up to me. "Father *thought* you might be angry! He feels now that he shouldn't have interceded for me. I feel *terrible*, Maximilian! Why can't I *ever* do anything right—why can't I fit in?"

"*I'm* not your shrink." I stepped up my pace.

"Maximilian, Father wants to know if you will go to the Kit Car Show tomorrow with him. Will you?"

I stopped. "The Kit Car Show? In Los Angeles?" She nodded, and I did some fast thinking. "What time?" Justine had served out her sentence, and we were to meet at ten for our first biking date since Aunt Celeste grounded her.

"At ten, he decided, because you have to go to work in the late afternoon." There were violet half-moons under her eyes—insomnia circles, Mom calls hers, which are dark gray. Burke's exactly matched her eyes, and gave her a tortured look, like an El Greco in last semester's art appreciation class.

"Burke, how about Sunday instead? Will the show still be on?"

"Father and I are to attend an informal chamber music recital—friends of mine. Of course Angelica will insist on coming too, although it will take all of her creativity to keep from looking bored." She sounded annoyed.

I was still punching keys on my mental computer. Maybe

Dad and I could go to the car show together on Sunday; no, not after that last Sunday—at UCLA. "I don't know, Burke. I sort of have—plans for Saturday."

She nodded briskly. "I know. Justine. I have already spoken to her about this."

"You have already *what?* What am I, anyway,—community property?"

"But I *knew* you would want to go to the show! I was only trying to pave the way for you, Maximilian!" Her eyes had opened wide in dismay.

"Listen, Burke, I'm not looking for someone to manage my life. But if I ever do, it isn't going to be you, so butt out, will you?" My voice was tight with barely concealed fury.

"Now then, do you see? Despite my best intentions, I simply can't do *anything* right! My peers all hate me, except for Justine!" A thin ribbon of tears trickled down each pinched cheek. How did she manage to send me on these guilt trips, anyway? I felt like Simon Legree, and impulsively reached out a hand to console her. She jumped back and screamed, and it was all I could do to keep from hitting her, instead.

"Princess! Over here! What's the matter?"

We were at the traffic circle, and Father Lindstrom and the boat-tail beauty were right on time. I walked around to the driver's side. "She's all right, sir. It's my fault—I almost *touched* her." I couldn't keep the annoyance out of my voice, but at the same time I felt a twist in my gut.

He looked at me sympathetically, then opened the door and got out of the car. *"You* take the wheel, Maximilian." He walked around to the other side, ushered Burke into the back seat, and got in beside me.

A thrill was running up and down my spine, making the

hairs on the back of my neck prickle. Driving the Auburn was the closest I'd come to ecstasy, as they say in the old romance mags, since I got my electric train on Christmas morning eight years ago. I wrapped my hands around the warm oak wheel.

"How would you like to drive the Auburn to the Kit Car Show tomorrow, Maximilian? Burke *did* explain, didn't she?"

My answer was loud and clear. "Yes, sir, she did. Thanks, I really appreciate it, sir." I shifted into low gear, and we started moving on a cloud.

"Hey, sport! Where'd you rip off the gas buggy?" It was Bedford. The Hunk was standing on the curb, Justine lounging on his arm. She smiled and waved to me, but I scowled and stared straight ahead. We cleared the traffic circle and eased into the street.

"Justine really doesn't mind, about tomorrow," Burke said cheerfully, turning the screws. "She said she has lots to do."

"I—see she has," I said grimly. Rage had turned into a large lump in my throat.

Mr. Lindstrom said quickly, "You're a good driver, Maximilian. You keep your eyes on the road. I like that."

I managed to gulp, "Thank you, sir. It's because of my dad—he still thinks he has to sit beside me, coaching me every time I take the car out."

"Well, when you ask your parents' permission to go tomorrow, be sure to tell them you'll be driving part of the way, and that I'll be right beside you."

"Right, Mr. Lindstrom. No problem, seeing it's you— Burke's father." I was struck by a debilitating thought. "Burke, are you coming tomorrow?" Maybe I had accepted too soon.

She said sharply, "I understand that plans were already made for me. Lanny Van Alston is coming over."

"Well, now, Princess—the Kit Car Show doesn't sound quite like your sort of day, anyway. And Lanny said he had a big surprise for you," Mr. Lindstrom said soothingly.

"I'll just bet he has. He plans to paw me, as usual." I was always unprepared for this Snow Cone candor. I kept forgetting that she said what she thought, not what she thought you wanted to hear.

"The surprise he mentioned to me was definitely not of that sort. Think positive, Princess. You're going to like it, I can assure you. But I promised not to tell. It's *his* surprise." He sounded confident.

"I'm *not* going to like it!" Burke shouted.

Out of the corner of my eye I noticed her dad smiling. "You'll see, Princess." He turned to me. "Maximilian, we're going to have a great time tomorrow. We'll be seeing some of the most stylish exotics and vintage replicars and kit cars in the country."

I put myself in the picture, behind the polished walnut wheel of the prettiest little burgundy '52 MG-TD that ever masqueraded as a yellow '67 VW Bug. Maximilian Murphy: Miming the Great Gatsby!

As if the drive to the show wasn't heady enough, the show itself blew me away, even though I hadn't quite forgotten last night's ominous phone conversation.

"But yes, cher!" Justine's dulcet tones had come too sweetly through the earpiece. "Burke has told me about the car show! I have always known that you love cars best!"

"Come on, Cherie! It's no fun to kiss a car! It's just that . . ."

"Oh, but do not worry, Maximilian! I am *very* busy!"

"You're very busy going out with *him,* aren't you—Bedford." I tried to assume my cool, man-of-the-world role.

"Only tomorrow night, Maximilian!" I could tell she was smirking into the mouthpiece.

I blew my cool. "Tomorrow *night!* But your aunt has always said . . ."

"Tante Celeste says Brad is more up-scale than . . . than. . ."—I tensed—"than most high-school boys. Brad, my Tante Celeste says, is like a *college* man! He has a red Accord, him!"

"Ha!" I screamed into the mouthpiece. "And she *trusts* college men? Doesn't she know what goes on in the squinched-up back seats of red Accords? More fool your Aunt Celeste!"

"Maximilian, you are calling my Tante Celeste bad names! Goodbye, you!" There was a click. I stared at the receiver. I was driving her straight into the Hunk's back seat.

The memory of the disastrous dialogue did a fast fade as Mr. Lindstrom and I walked onto the floor of Exhibit Hall Number Two of the Los Angeles Convention Center. Scott Fitzgerald might materialize at any moment, drink in hand, Zelda (in fringed dress and beaded headband) in tow. "Yes, sir, that's my baby . . ." was spilling happily from the loudspeakers spotted around the hall. We were in a time warp, and all the partygoers of the Jazz Age had parked their cars here in front of us: elegant Jaguars, timeless Rollses, frisky Model T's—Austin-Healeys, Cords, sporty Bugattis, MG's—dozens of MG's!

"You can close your mouth now, Maximilian." Mr. Lindstrom was smiling at me. "You'll have hours to enjoy. Shall we synchronize our watches—and meet here at two-thirty? That should get you home in time to get to work."

He vanished in the direction of an Auburn-Cord exhibit, and I had no trouble spotting the classic MG-TD's. I checked out the Rogue, the Gatsby Roadster, the Piccadilly, the Pacesetter, and finally the Country Lane, my freebie plastic tote bag bulging with brochures and flyers.

The Country Lane sales rep walked over to me, as I stood ogling the little burgundy beauty on its round display stand. "Isn't she a sweetheart? She has a pre-gel-coated body . . ."

I heard a sudden whirrr, then a muted thunk! right behind me. I whirled. Teitelbaum the Terrible was doing a toe stand on skates, inches from my feet.

"Trinka! What are *you* doing here? And how come you didn't knock me down—I thought that was the scenario!"

She was helpless with laughter, but she finally got control. "It's a gift! Imagine seeing *you* here, Maxie!"

She was decked out, as you'd expect, in fake fur: white fox bikini pants and bra, both of which were too small, as usual, but somehow tasteful, as they say, and white fox knee pads. She looked—well, foxy. She was improving with age. Her round face didn't exactly look fat any more; it was set off by a circle of dark curls, and dark eyes you might call merry. She carried a plastic bag over one arm.

"Haven't I seen you around the hall before?" the rep asked admiringly, his eyes moving up and down and sideways.

"You should have! I'm Miss Kit Car Show—I got the job on my looks and my talent!"

"And you deserve it, Miss Kit Car! Say, are you free for dinner—six o'clock?" His eyes had settled on her bosom, which of course overflowed the bikini top.

"No, I cost a lot!" She almost toppled over after that one. "So, Maxie, we meet again! Does that tell you anything?"

I grinned. "Sure. We can't keep on meeting like *this*, Trink. Not if you want me to keep on falling for you, as they say!"

"Maxie, Maxie!" My wit seemed to destroy her, and I wondered why I had always thought of her as a klutz. She dipped into her plastic bag and handed me some brochures and coupons. "Fill them in and drop the stubs in any exhbit box. Win yourself a couple of Bearcats, Bud!"

"Wow!" Think *lucky*, Maximilian!

"On with the show!" She blew me a kiss and skated off, backwards.

"Be careful, Miss Kit Car!" the rep called. "Friend of hers?" I nodded, and he hustled a garden chair over to me. "Have a seat! Can I get you some coffee?"

I shook my head. "Thanks, no. But I'd like to look over the car."

"Help yourself! Get in it—try it on for size!"

It was a perfect fit. I sat behind the walnut wheel on a soft, sand-colored (almost pink) vinyl seat, my eyes rising over the handcrafted walnut instrument panel to the rich burgundy of the hood, with its distinctive eagle ornament. Justine, of course, sat beside me, her head on my shoulder, her silky hair blowing in the wind against my cheek. She was dressed all in pink, a ruffly outfit with matching parasol. I was wearing goggles and a Gatsby cap and a duster, and it felt as though we were rolling along at ninety miles an hour. The big speedometer on the dashboard said only thirty. I had just taken my right hand off the wheel and put it around her shoulders, drawing her closer, when a movement outside caught my eye.

It couldn't be—but it was—a mime! I got out of the car, gently closing the door. He came up and stood next to me, a tall guy all in black except for white gloves and the mime face. There was something familiar about that face: the two vertical black grease-pencil lines slashing just one eye, the black tear rolling from the other, a black Chaplinesque mustache above a thin red line of a mouth. My mentor—it had to be!

"Kenny Power Wilson?" I held out my hand.

"Power Wilson. Right. So you're my public—I was wondering what had become of it!" He studied me, shaking my hand.

"Don't you remember me—Maximilian Merriwether Murphy—the kid that followed you all around Sand Hill Park at that fair in Belview Beach, two years ago? Hey, man, you changed my whole life!"

"There've been a lot of gigs, man. Not a lot of bucks, but fringe benefits—you know, like free goldfish for netting the suckers for the Dunk-a-Butt booth. Man, have I got an aquarium that just won't quit. What'd you say your name was?"

"Max." He had forgotten me. Murphy's Law.

"Right, Max. Say, man, you're going to have to get off this whirlybird. I'm about to do my silent sales pitch, and when I kick this little old button here on the floor this platform's going to start going in circles. So what else is new? What goes around comes around, right, Ted?"

I stepped down from the platform, suddenly depressed. He must have seen my tragic mask. Just as the MG-TD started to slowly revolve, he called, "Hey, Ted, hang around for an hour, will you? We can talk about old times, over a corn dog at the snack booth. Okay?"

When he'd come full circle, I nodded glumly. "Sure, okay, Kenny."

"Power. Catch my act now, Ted!"

"Say, you get around!" the sales rep said. "He's a friend of yours, too?"

I nodded. "I've known *him*—for two years."

"May as well sit down." He indicated the garden chair, and I sat down. "He's good—he'll be pulling an audience from all over the building, in seconds flat. Not a bad investment. He brought me two sales yesterday."

I had to know—it could mean my future. "How much of an investment?" I took him by surprise.

"Well, ah—he set his own scale—twenty-five bucks a day, two shows. The price is right. He works several other exhibits here, too."

Twenty-five big green ones a day, from this one gig! Now if he does even two others—that's seventy-five a day. Big bucks! Seventy-five a day for a week (make that six days, a guy needs one day off). I punched the "times" button on my mental calculator and came up with four hundred and fifty a week on the readout. Times four for a month—hey, man, a cool eighteen hundred! Easy street. Next month I'd take the California Proficiency test. Real world, here I come!

Suddenly I realized I was surrounded. The rep was right. Kenny—er, Power, was pulling them in. I watched, feeling a sense of awe creeping over me. Kenny Power Wilson was America's answer to Marcel Marceau!

He had black rubber legs and no spine. I caught my

breath as he bent backwards across the Country Lane's glossy hood, bringing his legs up and over his head to land on one leg, the other pointing skyward. A gymnast! He folded up into a cocoon, a faceless black cylinder that turned into an undulating butterfly. I'd worked on a butterfly routine, but that certain magical grace eluded me. Power flitted around the car, finally "flying" into the driver's seat, alighting on his toes, gently fluttering his "wings." A ballet dancer! I clapped as though I'd never seen another mime act.

Now he got into his audience interaction. He had a good eye—he chose a luscious blonde in a lavender velour jogging suit. He must have hit the floor button again, because the platform stopped as he took her hand. It started after she stepped up beside him, blushing and ducking her head. He pirouetted around the MG pointing out its features to her, and she began to relax and enjoy the show. He showed the boot in back where the vinyl top was stored along with the snap-in side curtains for rainy weather (you could almost see the raindrops as he moved his fingers), the big, shining chrome grill, the Country Lane medallion and car badges, the pretty upholstery. After he handed the girl into the driver's seat and closed the door, you almost hyperventilated keeping up with him as he ran frantically—in place—beside the car. It was a dazzling performance.

I was busy dissecting the act, stripping it down to its basic mime elements or essences so that I could understand exactly what made it work, when Power appeared beside me. "You like it, Ted?"

"Max. It was great! What can I say, Kenny—er, Power? You're the new Marcel Marceau!" I sounded like a kid at the zoo.

He laughed. "Come on. Let's hit up the snack bar for a corn dog—the mime machine needs refueling, even though it's tough to keep the mustard out of the mustache."

We lucked out and found a table-for-two in the refreshments pavilion. I got right to the point. "I'm going pro this summer, and I'd like to know the odds. You've got it made, Power—I figure you at eighteen hundred a month."

He almost dropped his cup of Kola King. "Just how do you figure *that,* mime?"

I explained my calculations and he leaned back on the wooden stool, miming wild laughter. When the silent fit subsided, he gasped, "Get off the dream machine, Ted! Get off cloud nine! Shake hands with the *real* world!"

I could feel my throat tightening. "Wait a minute, Power. You're the guy that turned me on to mime. I've been working at it ever since I saw *you* at the Sand Hill Fair in Belview Beach. I'm quitting school and going pro because of *you* . . . Are you trying to tell me I might not make it?"

He stopped clowning. It was a minute before he said anything. I waited—a knot in my gut. "Listen, Ted . . ."

"Max. Maximilian Merriwether Murphy."

"Okay, Max. Listen good. I've never seen you work. I don't know how good—or how bad—you are. So I'm not about to make some kind of stupid judgment, okay? I'll just tell you straight off—I don't work six days a week as a mime. I work six days a week as a dishwasher in the Seagull Cafe on Venice Beach. I've got a nice boss—a real okay guy—who lets me off the hook when a mime gig comes up for me. He understands. See, *he* wanted to be a jazzman all his life—he plays a mean horn, but he's sixty-two years old and he's still waiting for that big break. Get the picture?'' He finished off his corn dog, carefully dabbing at the fake mustache with a paper napkin.

I refused to believe the picture—it *had* to be out of focus. ''The Seagull Cafe? Hey, I did a routine on the sidewalk there, a few weeks ago! I did a basketball gig with Mile-High Mulligan. And a bicycle act, a street interaction—maybe you caught it?''

He shook his head. ''No way. I hang out with the help, Ted. In the back of the bus.''

''Hey, Power—you're a *great* mime! You ought to be doing commercials—on the tube! You're good enough!'' Until right now, I'd been planning to make out like a bandit, myself, on TV.

''Oh, right—commercials, every two-bit actor's fantasy, right? Sure, my agent's gotten me a turn or two—but do you know how many *good* mimes there are on the dream machine, Ted? Do you have any idea how many actors are out of work in tinsel town? But I'll tell you what, Ted— *I'm* going to make it if I have to wash dishes until *I'm* sixty-two—because I know my break's going to happen on *some* tomorrow! And I'll live in my roach-infested room in a moldy fleabag of a backwater hotel, ripping off cornflakes and eggs from the Seagull for my dinner, until I get the contract that will land me a condo in Beverly Hills!'' He looked at his watch. ''Let's go, mime. I'm on in a few minutes—I need a mirror first.''

We worked our way towards the john. ''Make sure you get a good coach,'' he said. ''That's where I put my money, on a good coach.'' I watched him push at the mustache with his index fingers as he stood before the mirror. ''I take my chances with the mustard—it's better than peeling off crepe wool—what this hairy stuff is made of.

Ever pull a mustache off the spirit gum? Takes half your face with it!'' He sharpened up the black tear with a black grease pencil, lengthened the parallel lines at the other eye, and drew a new mouth with a red pencil.

I walked with him back to the Country Lane exhibit.

''Catching my act again?'' Power said, just before he stepped up on the round platform. I nodded. ''Take the easy way out, mime.'' He smiled. ''Shoot yourself.''

★ ★ 14

The Snow Cone was sticking to me like a marshmallow on a toasting fork. I don't like marshmallows, and I'm not that big on Snow Cones, either. "So what did he give you?" I asked her curiously.

"What did *who* give me? And why do you want to know?" Burke looked at me with narrowed eyes. We were walking towards the traffic circle after school, and I was buoyed up by the certainty that I'd be rid of her within seconds now.

"That guy Lanny. You whined about him all the way home last Friday, when your dad let me drive the Auburn."

"Oh, Lanny. He gave me the Guarnerius." Her tone was matter-of-fact.

"Well," I said noncommittally, *"that* ought to make you happy.

"Very happy. But it wasn't really from Lanny. Ann-Oliveras bought it from a private party in Italy. This is the first time it has been out of its native land."

"Boffo," I said, conservatively. Then I threw caution to the winds, as they say. "Lanny's a great guy."

Her eyes slid over me—she was laughing inside. "I'm glad you like him." My ears were suddenly hot; she had

left me without a tag line. "Justine's a wonderful person,"
she added unexpectedly. Tit for tat, as they say, but she
sounded as though she meant it.

"I'm glad *you* like her." I didn't, at the moment. I was
still smarting from her latest Beford caper. Saturday *night!*

"But he brought me home at ten, *cher,* just like Tante
Celeste said, him!"

"Where'd you go? Did he kiss you? What happened?"
I demanded the morning after—Sunday—via Ma Bell, just
before carrying out my sentence for the day: spading up
the back yard for the new lawn.

"To a movie. This time, I did *not* let him. I have decided, I do *not* like his kind of kissing, me!" *That* was a
mixed review—I was both mad and glad. She was hurrying on with the report. "Tante Celeste, she likes Brad,
her! We had pecan pie and coffee and we all talked until,
oh, late, Maximilian! One o'clock yes?"

A pox on aunts and Accords . . .

"Do you know she has invited me to come to Louisiana
with her during spring break?" Burke turned and faced
me, her violet eyes flashing sunbeams, even though the
day was gray with winter overcast.

I swallowed a gasp. "We're—going to make quite a
California contingent." I said it lightly, with great effort.
"She invited *me* a long time ago."

"Well, *you've* never said you're going, Maximilian. She
says you won't spend the money, because you're saving
for a car. Of course that's a very worthwhile objective, but
I'm afraid Justine doesn't see it that way."

"What did she say—exactly?"

Burke looked at me closely. "Maybe I should tell you,"
she said after a moment. I braced myself. "She wanted
you to meet her family and see the bayou country. She's

very proud of it all, and she's very proud of you, Maximilian. Do you know that?''

"No. No, I didn't know she's—proud of me." I wanted to ask, why? And how come I didn't know? And why don't Justine and I ever talk about the things that really matter?

Burke smiled. "It isn't just your performing talent, Maximilian. She's proud of you for being—well, you. And she's disappointed that you don't want to go.''

"She said that? You're not improvising?'' My glance held hers.

"You know I never improvise.''

"I don't know where she got the idea I didn't want to go." I smiled at her. "Thanks, Burke—you've just sorted out my priorities. How about you? Are you going, *too?*''

"Of course. The invitation fits my plans, and timing, perfectly, Maximilian. Father and I—and Angelica is threatening to come too—will be in New Orleans that first weekend to hear a newly formed chamber group. I also intend to visit Preservation Hall in the Vieux Carré just because its jazz is seminal.''

I didn't know about seminal jazz, but I picked up on *parents*. "Your dad—and maybe your mom—are going with you? Are you *all* staying at Justine's?'' The Great Houma Escape was beginning to sound more like the jail-house blues.

"I don't know how it will work out—if Angelica comes!'' She suddenly looked distraught. "She practically *never* lets me out of her sight! *If* she comes, she'll spoil my entire cultural experience!'' She was at it again, collecting "experiences" the way my navy blue jacket collects Fat Cat's hairs. "Of course she'll come to hear me

in Houston. She'd never miss a chance to criticize me!''
We'd come to the traffic circle. Burke looked around, dismayed. The white and gold Auburn wasn't there.

"Hey, you're a big girl now," I said quickly. "You can
make it home on your own . . .''

She almost panicked as a low-slung blue job with a wide
chrome grin drove up and stopped beside us.

"Surprise, beautiful one!'' Lanny Van Alston unwound
from the curb-high driver's seat and stepped over to us.
His threads said ''preppie'' loud and clear, and several
girls in the vicinity stopped and stared, twittering and
squeaking like a miniature menagerie. His navy blue flan-
nels and matching turtleneck, topped by an Icelandic V-
neck sweater, weren't exactly from your friendly neighborhood Jacques Penné, as Justine calls J. C. Penney.
"Hello, Maximilian.'' We shook hands.

"Hi, Lanny. That's a little beauty there.'' I gestured
towards the car. "What is it?''

He laughed. *"This* is the little beauty, here.'' He smiled
at the Snow Cone. She didn't smile back. "The car's a
Maserati. Like a lift home?''

"Thanks, Lanny. I have to hang around here for a
while.''

"He's going to meet Justine,'' Burke said promptly.
"They make out almost every day after school, behind
metals shop.''

Wildfire swept over my ears—and my face. What *didn't*
she know? "Hey! Where'd you hear that?''

"Justine told me, of course,'' Burke said, smiling a secretive Mona Lisa smile.

It was unsettling. Somebody had a big mouth. Seething
inside, I laid plans to cut it down to size.

Lanny laughed. "Well, good for you, Maximilian! Good luck, old buddy—although it seems you already have it!" He gave Burke a longing look.

"I'm not going home with you, Lanny," Burke said, moving away from him. "I'm going to wait right here for Father. You could have saved yourself a long drive."

"Carter isn't coming, sweetheart. He's off at a conference at the Bonaventure, downtown. And Angelica suddenly flew off to Las Vegas to meet a new client—I drove her to the airport. She'll be back on the eight o'clock flight. I'm glad to fill in." She took another step away from him. "Shall we step into my chariot before it turns into a pumpkin, lovely lady?" He followed her.

"Don't you touch me, Lanny Van Alston! I'm going to *walk* home!" She ran towards the street, but Lanny sprinted after her and caught her easily. He scooped her up under one arm the way I do Fat Cat when he's heading for my room, the better to sharpen his claws on my newly upholstered reading chair.

There was a muffled scream as Lanny managed to clap a hand over her mouth, and hurried back to the car with her. I watched, impressed—and a little scared. I wasn't sure about this cave-man gig. How much did Lanny Van Alston *really* know about Burke Lindstrom?

One of her wildly kicking feet caught him in the knee. He yelled, "Ouch! Easy there! I promised your father I'd take care of you, lady! Open the door, Maximilian, please."

I did, and he dumped her in. She started screaming on schedule. He jumped into the driver's seat and the Maserati took off like a jack rabbit. As it whipped around the traffic circle I could see he had one arm firmly around Burke. He bent over her briefly—a kiss?—just before the car shot into the street. She'd be sick for a week. I tried to shrug it off.

"Is she being kidnapped?" a girl in a yellow jogging suit asked, her eyes wide with awe.

"He can kidnap *me* any time!" a little pigtailed freshman type said, sighing.

I shook my head. "No problem." I hoped I sounded more confident than I felt. "They're old friends. It's just a—*kid's* game they play."

She'd be all right, I told myself. That Lanny is an okay guy. Still, he was going to be alone with her at her house . . . On the other hand, a guy in his position had too much to lose . . . I suddenly realized I was replaying Burke's speech to me about Brad and Justine. I hurried toward metals shop.

"So, Maximilian—where you have been?" Justine was waiting for me at our bench. She stood in that familiar, aggressive pose—feet apart, hands on hourglass hips, bosom (as they call it in the old confession mags) pushed out. She was in the pink today: pink jeans, T, shoes, and jacket. My determination to take her to task threatened to jump ship.

"So," I countered, struggling to wrest my good sense back aboard, "Where have you been talking, Little Miss Mouth? Burke Lindstrom knows all about our—our rendezvous here. How come, and it better be good!"

"Oh, you, Maximilian!" She laughed a careless, tinkling laugh, shaking her head. "I *had* to tell her, *cher!* She keeps inviting me to come home with her after school, her!" She may have thought that explained it. Her hair fell in long ripples below her waist, shining even in the overcast.

"Don't *cher* me, you—you—beautiful little snitch!" I

grabbed her in a long, tight embrace. "How come you invited Burke to Houma, traitor?" I murmured into her hair.

"But she is a friend, Maximilian! And I am sad for her—she looks all the time like—white rice, her! Cajuns like *dirty* rice, Maximilian—with color: chicken livers and gizzards and oysters and onions!"

"So she's a friend," I persisted, skipping the recipe. "Have you forgotten three's a crowd? Especially when number three is Burke Lindstrom?"

"But you are not coming, Maximilian!" She reared back, her eyes narrowed, affording me a good view of her new shocking pink T.

"A fallacious assumption," I said casually. "Of course I'm coming. I wouldn't miss out on meeting your family for all the cars in the kingdom. If the rest of the Landrys are like the sample, I'll love 'em, you better believe."

"Maximilian!" She looked like pink cotton candy. "Oh, *cher,* you are saying yes, yes?"

"Yes." I kissed her. "So translate the new T. What's it say?"

" *'Laissez les bons temps rouler.'* That means, let the good times roll, yes, Maximilian?"

"You bet!" I covered her mouth with mine. The Bug was fading from the picture, but biking is good for the heart, as they say.

"Do I read you, Max?" Dad said at the dinner table. "Do you really plan to spend two hundred hard-earned bucks flying off to Louisiana on some harebrained expedition into the swamps? It's that girl, isn't it—you're after that girl hook, line, and sinker, that's it, isn't it? You get her pregnant, Max, and see how much help you get from your mother and me! Ha!'' He stabbed a piece of his roast beef viciously.

"Now, Quentin," Mom said, "I think you're overreacting. If Max wants to spend the money he's earned on a trip, I think that's his choice."

"Don't be naive, Annie! He's saving for a car, and he'll need it when he goes off to college! He doesn't know his own mind! This little skirt's put the blinders on him! Don't think I don't know boys!'' He took another swipe at the roast beef and nearly chased it off the plate.

"Quentin, dear," Mom said, passing the mashed potatoes. "Maximilian has to learn to make decisions sometime. He's growing up and you won't be able to save him from himself *all* his life, you know."

"*Some*body's got to save a stupid, wet-behind-the-ears, corn-green kid from himself, Annie! Look what he's trying to do—quit school, get a girl pregnant, mess up his whole life! And I couldn't care less! Let him! Pass the gravy, Max!''

I noticed his face was beet red. He cared. He *really* cared. I passed the gravy, as guilt settled over me like a hair shirt, as they say.

Mom casually dropped a bomb. "I called Justine's aunt today."

"Hey, Mom—you didn't! I'm not ten years old any more! I don't think you ought to be checking up on me!"

"Well, you *need* checking up on!" Dad shouted. "And if you don't keep a civil tongue in your head when you're talking to your mother, you're going to get a good cut across the butt! I *know* where the razor strop is now!"

"Miss Trahan assured me that the Houma trip would be very well supervised," Mom continued calmly. "And it really does sound interesting. She told me about the Landry family—they sound very close. And the culture must be fascinating—crawfishing and shrimping and hunting and big oil, and the marshes and bayous. It could be quite a worthwhile educational experience for Max, dear.''

"Is Tante Cel—Miss Trahan coming *too?*" The expedition was getting a bit unwieldy. We'd be sleeping in bunk-lined barracks like boy scouts. It wasn't my idea of heaven in Houma.

"Oh, no. She said there will be quite a houseful with just the immediate family. Imagine nine boys!''

"I can't,'' Dad said sourly.

"But she says they don't all live at home,'' Mom added.

"Well, the Sno—I mean, Burke Lindstrom and her father and maybe her mother are going,'' I said calculatingly.

"Really?'' Mom looked up from her asparagus, a Henry's Market eighty-nine-cent special. The usual two-dollars-a-pound was too rich for the Murphy blood. "Why, that's good news. I can't imagine Burke having that much free time.''

"It's a business and pleasure trip for her,'' I said, pouring it on. "She's going to go to a music gig in New Orleans first, then afterwards she'll be playing her big concert in Houston.'' I got carried away. "I plan to go to that—I mean, if you let me make the trip, Dad. This concert is supposed to be really big time. Abe Aaronson just wrote it up *again* in the *Times.*"

"Hmmmf," Dad snorted. He waited a beat. "So where will *you* stay, in Houston?''

I felt my spirits soar, as they say, leaving the hair shirt behind. "I figured I'd stay in whatever hotel the Lindstrom's stay in.'' It was creative thinking.

"Fifty bucks a night single!" Dad said warningly.

I gulped. "Well, yeah. Last of the big spenders."

Dad stood up. "So with your poke busted wide open, you'll be going on with school, I presume, Mr. Independently Wealthy?" He impaled me on his stare.

I was quiet for a moment. "I—think—I can make it on my own, Dad. I know a guy who can probably get me a job in a restaurant. He's a mime, too. A good one."

"So this big talent is washing dishes or working for tips, right? If this is the way your super-mime is making it big, how do you think Mr. Mediocre is going to come off, Max? Thought about it?" His voice was getting louder.

"Now, Quentin," Mom said, "I can see you're getting ready to issue one of your ultimatums. I wish you wouldn't."

"If wishes were horses, Annie, beggars would ride!" Dad shouted, galloping off on another trite Murphy truism. "The point is, this kid doesn't know *what* he wants! But *I* know what he *needs*—and that's a firm hand! And he's going to get it—right now!"

"Now, Quentin. Think about it first."

"I've already thought about it!" Dad roared. "Now you hear this, Max Murphy, and listen good! You're going to get an education *first* and *foremost* and that means staying in school! Furthermore, you're going to forget that girl, as of now, even if I have to send you to military school clear across the country! Clear?"

Furious, I jumped up from the table and faced off. "And what if I *don't* stay in school—and forget Justine? Just what can *you* do about it?" Now *I* was shouting.

He headed for the bedroom. "I'll show you what I can do about it! Since when do you get off smart-mouthing your father?"

"Quentin," Mom said firmly, and Dad stopped in his tracks. "You will please forget that old strop, dear. And Maximilian, you will please apologize to your father for your inexcusable rudeness. Right now."

"Hey, Mom . . ." I wasn't about to.

"Right now, Maximilian."

"Okay, okay." I said begrudgingly to Dad, "I'm sorry."

"You will please clean up your act, Maximilian." Mom looked straight at me. The general was pulling rank again.

"Well—okay, okay, Mom." I walked over to Dad. His eyes looked tired, and his shoulders slumped. He was getting old and I hadn't noticed it before. "Dad, I really am sorry. I wish I could see things—your way. I guess I just can't. I'm sorry." I held out my hand.

I thought for a minute he was going to deck me. Then he grabbed me in his arms and held me in a bear hug for several long moments, his head against mine. Suddenly he let me go, with a slap on the back.

"Time for 'Today on Wall Street,' " he said gruffly, turning away.

"Mind if I watch with you, Dad? Maybe I can pick up—a high-yield tip or two. I can sure use it!" I looked at him uncertainly. My smile felt crooked.

The corners of his eyes glistened. Then he smiled back. "Come on, son."

"Mox, this is my goodbye run. I won' see you again, I don' think." The Rabbit had slowed, to let me catch him.

I hauled up short. We were about at the halfway point in our Friday morning workout. Tomorrow morning at seven, Justine and I would be flying to Houston. We had our tickets, and now I was about two hundred big ones poorer.

"Hey, Rabbit—you aren't serious!" I could feel my mouth come unhinged. "What's happened? Has the INS caught up with you?"

"No, Mox. My mama is sick—she cannot work no more. We have to go back to Mexico. We go tomorrow on the bus."

I stopped stock-still, as they say, on the crest of the sand hill. The Rabbit jogged back to me. "Hey, Rabbit, you can't do that! You can't just give up your big chance! Three college coaches are fighting for you! You'll get a free ride, Rabbit! You *can't* quit *now!*" I was aghast. The Rabbit's future was in the bag—the scouts found him just two days after the Kola King Marathon.

The Rabbit shrugged. "My mama is sick, Mox. We have to go home."

"Well, can't she get a doctor *here?* Why do you have to go all the way back to *Mexico?*"

"My mama is afraid of trouble, Mox. We stay away from doctors an' lawyers an' cops, all those guys. Don' worry, Mox. I will run in Creel just the same, up an' down real mountains."

I wasn't impressed. So who'd *see* him running around those mountains? Not the judges at the Olympic trials.

"Wait a minute, Rabbit! You don't *have* to go! My dad says you can get a student visa to go to school *here!* Holy Sacramento, you can stay with *us!*" The fact that my future as one of *us* was pretty shaky at this point had momentarily slipped my mind.

The Rabbit smiled patiently. "I have to get the student visa when I am in *Mexico,* Mox. You think the INS is going to tell this wetback, 'Sure, Wetback, you sneaked in, but we will fix it all up for you. *Bienvenido!* Welcome!' You think so, Mox?" I just stood there, fast sinking into mental quicksand, so he went on. "Anyway, my mama cannot go home alone. I will go with her, on the bus. She needs me to take care of her."

"But that's got to be a long, long trip on a bus, Rabbit! If your mom is *that* sick, she could get *worse* before you get to Cray-el!"

"It is not so long a trip. Maybe three days to Los Mochis, if the bridges have not wash' out again. Then the Chihuahua and Pacific train will take us home in maybe six, seven hours, Mox."

"Well, Holy Toledo, as they say, Rabbit! That sounds terrible! Just how sick *is* your mom?"

"She cannot walk too good, and one side of her face, it don' work no more. So she cannot talk so good or eat so good. But she is a very brave woman.'' He stood tall, for a short guy.

''Well, sure she is! But you can't let her make a tough trip like that! You've got to *fly!* That way you'll get her there all in a day or so!''

''Well, Mox, we don' have wings, and we don' have money, so we take the bus. Don' worry.''

I was hit by a haymaker of an idea—Dad would demote it from inspiration to impulse, but there's a fine line there. Without thinking twice, violating still another Murphy maxim, I said, ''You're flying. I'm buying the tickets, and one of them is going to be round-trip. You're coming back, Rabbit, and that's the *only* way you can pay me back, understand? Hey, I don't want to blow the chance to be the running buddy of the next Olympic gold medalist in the marathon, the ten-thousand meter, the five thousand— you name it, you've got it!'' I thrust out my hand. ''Shake on it!''

The Rabbit looked at me impassively. I stood there for a long minute with my hand stuck out, before he took it.

Then he started running. ''Come on, Mox! We're only jus' halfway home!'' We took off like a couple of F-15s on a mission.

I went to the bank right after school and withdrew the rest of my savings, all but one dollar. I didn't want to close out the account. Maybe that one buck would lure other bucks, or split up like amoeba.

I met the Rabbit at Sand and Sea Travel Service.

''I cannot do this, Mox. Now you have no money. You have give it all to Mama and me.'' His head drooped, and I could hardly see his eyes under the shock of black hair. ''I don' know *when* I can pay you back, Mox.''

I said with a forcefulness that surprised me, "Look, I told you, forget it! Just come *back,* okay? You're the only brother I've ever had." I straightened my shoulders. Brothers beat out VW Bugs.

That night I put in what I suspected was my last shift at the station. My boss had been underwhelmed by my travel plans.

"You know what I told you, Max. This time I've had to find a new hire for swing. I can't ask Del to work two back-to-back shifts two weekends in a row. Call me when you get back. If this kid works out, you're axed. Sorry, Max. But I warned you."

I didn't say anything. But what I *wanted* to say was, Yeah, Boss, but didn't *you* ever take a week off when you were sixteen? On the other hand, I don't think he had ever been sixteen—he was born forty. I felt more than depressed. I felt unappreciated. I *knew* I'd done a good job for the boss—and my shift was the dirtiest. Swing wasn't only tally and lock-up time, it was holdup and drunk-driver time.

It had been a crazy day—from airplanes to alligator gumbo, both a first for me. I hoped the 'gator stew would also be a *last;* I'd found the meat a bit too tough to be toothsome.

"That Albert!" Justine's mom had laughed that night, when we finally connected with her at the Houma street dance. "I'll bet he drove like a 'gator after a chicken neck, him!" Justine's oldest brother had picked us up at the Houston airport, and from there across the tail-end of Texas to the midsection of the French triangle in southern Louisiana, we had hardly touched rubber to roadway. We made one stop—to refuel the panting Ford pickup and ourselves.

It wasn't until after midnight, when my Louisiana lovely and I were mildly making out on the big wooden porch swing on what Justine called the gallery and I called the front porch, which ran clear across the front of the Landrys' house, that we got a chance to talk.

"You liked the street dance, yes, Maximilian?" I had my arms around her, my lips hovering above hers. Our feet were in sync, pushing the swing slowly back and forth to the tune of its rhythmic hoarse squeak.

"Sure, but I'd have liked it better if Albert hadn't scared me spitless getting us to Houma in time for it, and if *you* hadn't been up on that pedestal all night. I missed you, Dolly Parton." I kissed her. She had been the darling of the dance—discovered immediately, given a borrowed guitar, and lifted up on stage.

"Yes, but you *danced, cher.* I saw you and Maman, and you and that blonde, and she had her cheek right next to yours, that blonde, yes?" She glanced at me reprovingly.

"Your mom and I teamed up for a few Cajun kickers, true, Cherie. Those chanky-chank bands are real toe-tappers." I kissed the top of her head and let my eyes stroll across her pink T—although, since we'd been in these same threads for about twenty hours, I knew the message by heart: *Sauce Piquante.* I pulled her closer.

"That blonde girl, Maximilian," the Belle of the Bayou persisted, resisting me.

"Oh, *that* blonde. She's French-French from Paris. She says she's over here studying you quaint Cajuns and your fractured Frenglish."

Justine laughed softly. "Her! Well, I will study those funny French, them, in my junior year in college when I am in Paris."

She'd gotten my attention. I reared back, looking her in the eye, as they say. "Now wait a minute—just back up there. What's this about college? The scenario says we're into show biz, *you and me.*" My pushing foot jumped out of sync with hers, and the swing jerked to a stop. Symbolic, I thought darkly.

"*Brad* says, Brooke Shields is going to *Princeton,* her!"

" '*Brad* says' " I exploded. "Since when is he your guru?" It was a shocker—I thought I'd left the Hunk in Belview Beach.

"Shh!" Justine put her hand over my mouth; I grabbed it and held it tight. "*Brad* says that I am too smart, me, *not* to go to college, and if I go to *his* college, Brad says . . .''

"Forget what *Brad* says!" I struggled to keep my voice down. "Eve listened to the *snake,* too—zap, there went the old neighborhood!"

She started to giggle. "But Brad, he is not *funny* like you, *cher,* I guarantee . . .'' I stopped her giggling with a long, langorous, and strictly serious kiss. I had no intentions of being typecast as a clown.

"Not that your guarantees are worth a plugged nickel, as Dad says," I said, finally giving her a chance to breathe. "Look at your track record, Cherie: born in a cabin on the banks of the bayou, you said. Saving Christmas for three months, you said. What happened to all that stuff?''

She let her head sink back onto my shoulder, smiling secretly. "That stuff—is *almost* true! Just because Maman and my daddy jumped into the motor pirogue and hurried up the bayou to the hospital does not mean that I could *not* have been born in the trapper's cabin, yes? It was a good season for muskrat, *cher!*''

"So you were born in a hospital like everybody else, with or without muskrats. Now clear up Christmas." My arms tightened around her. Our feet were in sync again, and the swing was singing hoarsely.

"Just because once the boys did not get home from trapping in time for Christmas, because the 'rats and the nutria were so many that year, does not mean it could never happen again, yes?"

"Probably not, but pucker up anyway, *just because* I love you." Our lips were within an inch of meeting, when a treble squeak interrupted the swing's comfortable song. A door closed softly.

We both sat bolt upright. A small figure in cut-off pajamas was standing outside the front door, illumined by a sliver of moonlight drifting beneath the porch overhang.

"Ron-Guidry!" Justine said sharply to her littlest brother, who had canceled out his own name, Claude, in favor of that of the famous "Ragin Cajun" Yankee pitcher. "You're supposed to be asleep a long time ago!"

The little boy came towards us on bare feet. "We've been waiting for Maximilian to come home," he said sleepily, rubbing his eyes. "Charles and me, we have a bet, us. He says Maximilian will fall down when he tries to get in the top bunk, because we hid the ladder. But me, I say he's so tall he'll just step right into it from the floor, him. So hurry up and kiss her, Maximilian."

Justine said indignantly, "For shame on you, *cher!* Maximilian is company! He gets the best bunk—and that's the bottom one!"

"I think Charles is alseep in it," Ron-Guidry said doubtfully. "But he can have mine—the middle one."

"Ron-Guidry, you just find the ladder and make Charles climb up to the top bunk! For shame, for shame, *cher!* Now don't you make bets on Maximilian again, him!''

"But we can make bets on the dried toad, yes, Justine?'' the *enfant terrible,* as the French say, piped up. "I put it in your bed. Charles bet you'll scream when you lie down on it, but me, I bet you won't scream till morning when you see it, you.''

"You got it for me! Oh, I thank you, *cher!''* She jumped up impulsively from the swing to hug him and I landed with a thud on my rump.

Ron-Guidry squealed, "Oh, I win, I win! I bet Charles that Maximilian didn't know about the swing! I win!''

I picked myself up. Suddenly I had had it. It *had* been a long day's journey into night, as some guy said. "Come on, R-G.,'' I said wearily. "I bet I'll be asleep before you are.'' I was asleep right now.

"What'll you bet?''

"I'll bet you'll get a sore bottom if you don't leave Maximilian alone, him, Ron-Guidry!'' Justine looked irresistibly belligerent. I could almost forget my fatigue.

"All right! Then I won't tell him a girl called tonight!''

Justine and I looked at each other. Only one girl would be calling me in Houma—the girl in New Orleans. "Burke,'' I said. I turned to the little boy. "What did she want?''

"I can't remember,'' my bunkmate said calculatingly.

"You took the words right out of my mouth, R-G,'' I said. "I was just going to bet you a red balloon-dog you couldn't remember. I win. Give me a red balloon-dog.''

"I passed you a hot potato, *cher,''* he said, grinning.

"He means he was fooling with you, Maximilian.'' She gave him a little shake. "Go to bed, bad boy.''

"I win!" he said triumphantly. "She said she and her maman will be here tomorrow afternoon, them. She was crying. And a lady was yelling! I bet you don't even *have* a red balloon-dog, Maximilian!"

"You lose, R-G." I pulled one of the long, skinny balloons out of my jeans pocket, stretched it, and with weak lungs blew it up, then twisted it. Instant dachshund.

Something told me we were *all* about to be losers. The winged one was taking another bad header straight for us, like Marceau's angel in a downdraft. And the Snow Cone was going to drip acid rain all over our parade, a whole day early. Murphy's Law was still operational.

★ ★ *16*

The next day about noon, stuffed with *boudin*—hot, spiced Cajun sausage—and grits, Justine and I lolled at opposite ends of the big porch swing, convalescing from the previous long day and short night.

The Landrys had left for Mass before we got up, except for R-G and Charles. My bunkmates were off crawfishing in local ponds with their weird little wire and cotton-mesh dip nets. Two of their big brothers, the oystermen Thomas and Edwin, would be supplementing the boys' catch with gunnysacks of the little four-inch freshwater crustaceans. *En famille,* as the French put it, plus friends and neighbors, the Landry clan was holding a big crawfish boil in the backyard tonight.

"There will be bets on who can eat the most crawfish," Justine said, lazily sipping lethal Cajun coffee. I had tried it, and it was potent enough to make a strong man cry, as they say in the old *True Life Adventures*. It brought tears to *my* eyes, and I had hastily dumped out half a cup and filled it up with hot water. "Once Edwin ate twenty-five pounds of crawfish, but that is only ten pounds of meat, from the tail. He won."

"I'll bet he did!" I said, waking up. "*Ten* pounds of meat!"

"You squeeze the head, *cher,* and eat the tail," she said hungrily. "Because the head has the good fat, yes?"

"Being a fathead has *never* paid off," I said, subduing a shudder.

"But the tail," she went on with enthusiasm, "it is covered by a shell, and you must work *hard* for one bite of meat! The crawfish, he is a mean one, *cher.* He will fight to pinch you, him, until he gets dropped in the pot and turns red."

"Well, under the circumstances, you can hardly blame him for being mean, Cherie." I sighed over the fate of the crawfish.

"A car is stopping," Justine said, looking out towards the street. "It is maybe Burke."

Moments later, a familiar, pale figure in white started up the walk, wearing what the Bullock's Junior Miss would naturally wear on safari in the tropics, jaunty knee-length walking shorts and a soft cotton campaign shirt with rolled-up sleeves.

I stood up, just as though Dad were right there, watching. "Hello, Burke. How come you're a day early?" I wasn't pleased. Justine jumped up to throw her arms around the Snow Cone, and the treacherous swing shot forward, knocking me in the back of the knees. I forgot there were ladies present. "Curses!" I yelled.

Burke turned to face me, little tears starting from the corners of her eyes. "Maximilian, if you don't like me, it's more honest to just say so! I *thought* you were a friend!" It had a familiar ring.

I said quickly, "Hey, I *am!* We *are!* What's the matter with you anyway, Burke? You look—wasted."

"Maximilian, you are not being nice again, you." Justine shot me a reproving glance.

"But he's right. I *feel* wasted!" Burke said, nervously. *"Father* didn't come!"

"So I gathered." I looked at the blue Plymouth Reliant parked in front of the house. "Is that your mom in the car?"

"Yes! And I can't stand one single more day with her— or I won't be able to play next Saturday night! I need peace, and my own space! We're driving back to New Orleans later today and flying home tomorrow."

"What!" We said it together—me in relief. "You'll have to fly all the way back to Houston next weekend, then," I added cheerfully.

Justine cut in anxiously, "But you can't, Burke! You and your maman, you must stay here! The room is all ready for you, *chère!* And tonight there is the crawfish boil, and tomorrow we will go to the trapper's cabin on the bayou."

The winged one, here? I sent frantic ESP's to Justine to cool it.

"Oh, but Angelica *never* stays with other people! She *says* she doesn't want to impose! But it's *really* because she's totally self-centered and wants her privacy, especially her own private bath! And of course she'd *never* let me stay here alone!"

"Alone?" Justine said, surprised. "There's Maman and Daddy and Charles and Ron-Guidry and . . ."

Burke interrupted. "She means alone without *her!*" She dabbed at her eyes with a real handkerchief. I hadn't seen one of those since Mom gave away my grandmother's collection.

There was an awkward silence. I said, "Well, how was the concert?" Not that I cared.

"Disappointing. And Angelica was in a snit because we

had wasted our time! But *she* loathes even the *best* of chamber music—it's so *dispirited,* she says! Can you imagine? There's certainly nothing dispirited about Beethoven's Opus Eighteen, Number One! Why, the fugues alone . . .'' The handkerchief was getting soggy.

I pulled a Kleenex out of my pocket and handed it to her. "Here. Well, what about Preservation Hall? Did you get a charge out of that?"

The floodgates opened. "Preservation Hall was a disaster!" Her voice shook. "Oh, the music was marvelous! All those fabulous old jazz musicians—they're simply wonderful—so legendary!"

"So what went wrong?" I contributed another Kleenex.

"Angelica hated the *hall!* A dreary old tumbledown place, she called it! She *refused* to rise above it! She *despised* all the cigarette smoke, and the tacky young people sitting on pillows on the floor, and the rickety wooden chairs we sat on! It was *so* embarrassing, being dragged out through that hushed, worshipful audience!" Two sharp honks cut in, and Burke screamed towards the street, "Oh, just a minute, Angelica! Can't I talk with my friends for even one moment?"

Justine put a hand on her arm. "We will ask her to come join us, *chère,* here on the gallery. She cannot depend on the swing, but she will like the rocking chair, her."

"She'll instantly hate it! She'd say it made her look old! No, we've come to take you both with us for a boat ride in the swamps, since I'm to miss out on everything else! We got the brochure at the tourist office in New Orleans, and they made reservations for us."

"But tomorrow we are *all* to go for a boat ride on the bayou . . ." Justine began.

"Oh, look, it's raining!" Burke said sharply, as if the weather were a blatant conspiracy.

"Hey, liquid sunshine, as we say in California!" I said with some forced cheerfulness. The cotton clouds of the morning had gone flat and graying.

"Oh, but Maximilian, it happens all the time in the south, *cher!* Soon it will be over."

I put my arm around her and gave her waist a secret squeeze. "I vote we wait for tomorrow."

Burke's voice rose to a scream. "Oh, isn't *any*body my friend? I feel so—alienated! I wish I'd never come! If only Father . . ." Three quick, sharp honks interrupted. "Stop it, stop it, Angelica!"

Justine looked pensive, as they say. "A penny," I offered.

"I am thinking, Maximilian. Today after church, friends are coming to see me. If I am not here, they will still have Maman's little cakes and lemonade and coffee and much talking. When I get back, the little cakes and lemonade will be gone, but there will still be coffee and more talking. We will go with Burke, us."

"What!" I said. "And miss the cakes?"

The short trip to the boat dock on Bayou Black, two or three miles outside of Houma, wasn't the happiest hayride I'd ever had, despite the fact that my cute Cajun and I were holding hands in the Reliant's back seat. It wasn't just the weather outside, although the rain came down steadily. The sky had turned dark and surly, and the air felt heavy with heat and humidity.

I was glad we'd traded our Sunday threads for cut-offs and T's, despite the chill inside the car. Mrs. Lindstrom,

frosty in faultless white linen, her varnished blonde page-
boy frozen against her shoulders, was an ice sculpture.
The Snow Cone sat rigidly staring into the rain.

Burke's mom finally broke the silence. "Have you been
having a good time in Louisiana, Maximilian?" It sounded
like a safe enough opener.

"Yes, ma'am," I said, smiling at Justine. She gave my
hand a squeeze.

"Tonight we are having a crawfish boil in our backyard," Justine said conversationally.

"In the *rain?*" Mrs. L's voice laid on the irony with a
trowel.

"It will not rain tonight, I guarantee," the Resident
Weather Lady said serenely.

"And tomorrow Justine had exciting plans for us!"
Burke said, suddenly angry. "Oh, if only *Father* . . ."

"You made the decision, Burke," her mother cut in
coldly. *"You* chose to fly home. It's just too bad you don't
know your own mind. Under the circumstances, you
shouldn't have insisted on coming to Louisiana in the first
place. You're such a *child.*"

"At least *you* choose to treat me like one!" Burke
shouted. "You've turned into the very *worst* of stage
mothers, Angelica! How many professionals have to drag
their *mothers* along with them everywhere, even to visit a
friend!"

"That's right, Burke. Hurt me. Just keep on hurting me.
You're doing a magnificent job. Here I am sacrificing my
work to satisfy your little Louisiana whim . . ."

"You mean, to make peace with your conscience!" Her
voice rose. "Well, you can't turn back the clock—I'm not
six years old and you can't undo what has been done!"

I noticed my mouth was half open. I shut it—I shouldn't

have been so astounded at a Lindstrom scene. But it wasn't the Murphy style—Mom saw to that. I glanced at Justine—her eyes were twice as big as usual.

"Ungrateful girl!" Mrs. L fairly spat out. "I'm trying so hard to make up to you for all those years . . ."

"Well, quit trying, Angelica! You're a *failure* at it! Oh, how I wish we could have gotten a plane out last night!"

"You would have missed your precious swamp experience, my girl! And you may anyway. I doubt if any boat would go out in this weather."

Justine leaned forward. "Please, Mrs. Lindstrom, you must turn right at the sign that says, 'Bayou Boat Tours'—just ahead."

"Thank you, Justine. If Burke hadn't been so disagreeable, I would have paid closer attention to the road."

Burke shouted, "Well, I didn't start it, Angelica!"

"Now you will be having fun, Burke," Justine put in hastily. "You will like the alligators, yes?"

I forced a cheerful laugh. "But maybe not as much as they'd like *Burke,* right?" It was my last bit of alligator levity for life.

★ ★ 17

The graveled road dead-ended at a frame house beside the bayou. As we got out of the car, the rain obligingly trickled to a halt. A big man, leaning on a cane, limped over to meet us.

"Ah, Justine!" He gave her a bear hug.

"Nonc Claren." She turned to us, smiling. "Nonc isn't really my uncle. But he is just like one, him!" She introduced us.

Nonc Claren gestured towards the house. "Come in, come in. Lucie made us a Mississippi Mud Cake before she took off for Lafayette. And there's coffee."

Minutes later we were sitting around the small living room spooning up pudding-soft chocolate cake. I demolished my dishful in seconds. Then I pretended to sip at my coffee.

Nonc Claren said, "Nice surprise, little niece. The lady here didn't say who her guests were when she made the reservation. Since you're one of them, there's no charge, you know. No, I wouldn't hear of it!" He held up a hand, as Mrs. L started to protest. "But there's a catch. *You* take the skiff out, honey—the one with the electric starter. My rheumatism is acting up again, you can see, and I'd like to save myself for a boatload I'm chauffeuring just before sunset, in the ski barge. I've already put the bag of chicken on board. Here you go." He handed her the keys.

"Nonc Claren! I thank you, *cher!*" She jumped up to hug him.

"But she . . ." Mrs. Lindstrom began, and Nonc smiled, interrupting.

"Don't worry, ma'am. Justine has been skippering for me since she was twelve years old. But I'm glad she's getting away from the swamps—maybe rheumatism won't catch up with *her*."

On the way to the boathouse I said, looking at the keys in her hand, "Hey, I didn't know you knew how to run a boat, Cherie."

She grinned. "There is much that you do not know about me, yes, Maximilian?"

"I'm willing to research it," I said in a low voice.

"Do you think the rain is over?" Burke asked uneasily, glancing at the sky.

"Maybe. And maybe, non, yes?" Justine shrugged. "Anyway there are always ponchos on the boat, *chère*."

Mrs. Lindstrom surveyed her disapprovingly. "You're very young, Justine. Are you certain you know how to handle a boat? Especially if something unexpected should happen?"

"When one grows up in the marsh, there are not too many surprises left, yes?" She smiled confidently. But she confessed later that, well, yes, there was at least one.

Burke stepped into the boat first, conspicuously choosing the bow seat, where she could sit alone. I shared the middle seat with her mom, and Justine manned the tiller and the outboard motor in the stern. We slid out from under the boathouse roof and were soon cruising among big tree stumps in a wide waterway. Trees overhung the banks, most of them festooned with gray Spanish moss.

"The moss," our guide was pointing out, "the Cajuns, they call it Spanish *beard,* and we used to use it to stuff mattresses and furniture. It grows on the cypresses. The willows, they bend, and the moss falls off, yes? You see these stumps?" You couldn't miss them—we were winding our way among them. They must have been giants, cut off at the ankles, but still challenging the right-of-way. "These are cypress stumps, them. The big trees, they are all gone; overcut a long time ago to make houses and ships' masts and pirogues. Cypresses are rot resistant and those stumps are as sound now as they were a hundred years ago, yes?" She paused, and I sat dumbfounded at Miss Ph.D. Landry. "In another hundred years, say the geologists," she said cheerfully, "this marsh will be gone. The whole of Terrebonne Parish will be gone. It is sinking into the Gulf—forty square miles a year are lost. Louisiana, it is disappearing, yes?"

"Yes, and so is California," I said regretfully. "I hope the East Coast holds."

"You must take a very good look at all this while it is still here," she urged, as though the distant thunder was actually an approaching apocalypse.

"I think I felt a drop of rain," Mrs. Lindstrom said, looking up at the sky.

"There are orange ponchos, beneath the seats. But now we are to go under a big green umbrella. Oh, it is beautiful in there, I guarantee!" Justine turned the boat into a shadowy channel with a vaulted ceiling of moss-hung trees. "Today we might not see the snakes. They like to lie in the sunshine and today there is no sun." She sounded apologetic.

"Snakes! Oh, it's dark and *spooky* in here! Snakes!" A shudder shook the back in front of me.

"Don't be childish, Burke," Mrs. Lindstrom snapped. "It's not as though you're out there swimming with them."

Burke turned to look at us—her face had taken on a reflected ghostly green. "I'm not much of a swimmer."

"Now we are soon leaving the jungle," our captain announced. "And we are going to the lake. It is a private place with a fence around it, so the poachers cannot get the alligators and the birds. See that line strung above the water there?" We glanced where she pointed. "See that piece of meat—I think it is chicken—in the middle of the line? There is a hook inside, yes? The alligator who jumps up to grab that bait, he is alligator gumbo tonight, him!"

"Oh, how repulsive!" Burke shivered. "I didn't know people ate alligators!"

"Oh, but I will tell you a funny thing we Cajuns say about ourselves, us! A Cajun, he is someone who eats *any*thing before it eats him! But I think that is not just a Cajun—it is a Maximilian!" She laughed merrily, and I felt obligated to join in. The Lindstrom ladies sat in frozen silence.

Justine pointed the blunted prow toward a large patch of water lilies. Burke leaned over to touch one of the large waxy flowers. "How beautiful!"

Justine said quickly, "Oh, but you must keep your hands inside the boat, Burke! Alligators like fingers just as much as they like frogs or fish."

Mrs. Lindstrom leaned forward, obviously alarmed. "Oh, darling, be careful!"

Burke turned, startled. "I can take care of myself." I noticed the hurt look in her mom's eyes.

Justine held up a hand, testing the weather. "But yes,

it is going to rain. Do not forget the ponchos. Me, I will not wear one—plastic, it is too hot, and the rain, it is soon gone. Burke?'' Burke turned. "Here is the key to the lock on the gate. Now we will go into the private preserve. Please, you will open the gate when I get the bow of the boat up against it, yes, *chère?*''

"Let Maximilian do it,'' Mrs. Lindstrom said tightly as I passed the key on its yellow flotation ring up to Burke.

"Oh, for heaven's sake, Angelica! Can't you *ever* leave me alone?''

The boat crept slowly forward and stopped at the wide gate. I could see wire fencing running through the marsh on each side. "Now, Burke. Please,'' Justine ordered.

Burke leaned so far over the bow to reach the gate I began to think negatively myself. "Watch out!'' her mother screamed, while I held my breath.

"Angelica! You almost made me fall in! It would have been your fault!'' She glared at her mother, passing the ring back. "It's open. Here's the key.''

"I thank you, *chère*. We will leave it open until we come back out. Now, everybody, hold tight to your seats, please. I am gunning the engine so we fly right over these hyacinths that are filling up the lake, them! Now we go!''

The boat shuddered then skimmed over the lily pads like a dragonfly, as Justine throttled the motor, then idled back and tilted the propeller up out of the water. We were soon in a large, silvered lake reflecting the mirror image of the island in the middle. It was too early in the day for the thousands of birds that flew in each evening to overnight in the safety of the island, Justine explained—herons and snowy egrets and the spoonbilled flame birds. "So, now we will go find the babies.''

The babies, it turned out, were the alligators. The boat

idled to a stop in a cove carpeted by pastel water lilies. "Now, we must be quiet, and I will call the babies, just like Nonc and Tante Lucie." We scarcely breathed. "Dolly—come, Dolly!" She tapped the side of the boat. "Timmy, over here, you! Clinton! Come! Dinner, babies!" She waited a beat, then repeated the call. Minutes later, while our eyes searched the water eagerly, she pointed out into the lake. "There. See?"

"Where? Where?" I whispered.

"Is that an alligator—that looks like a half-submerged log?" Burke pointed.

"Oh, yes, Burke," Justine agreed. "That is a log—with eyes, watching us! Once, a long time ago, hunters used to cruise the bayous with lanterns, at night. Red eyes glowed along the banks like little coals. The lanterns, they made the 'gators—hypnotized, yes? And the hunters walked right up to the poor Timmys and Dollys while they watched, and knifed them or shot them between the eyes."

"Oh, terrible—terrible!" It was a low cry from Burke, accompanied by a shudder. Her mother sat stiffly silent.

"Yes," Justine readily agreed. "Then when there were not enough eyes left along the banks, the hunters began poling the 'gators. They would follow the tracks right to the dens, then reach in with long hooked poles, and pull the 'gators out. But if the hunter was not a good shot, him—that 'gator had *people* gumbo for dinner." She paused. "Shh! Here he comes! Hello, Timmy baby! You have come for your nice chicken dinner, yes?"

She draped the meat over one end of the pole and held it over the water. Timmy circled a few times, while Burke whispered, "How do you know that one's Timmy?" The alligator stretched for the meat, and swam off with a slap of his tail. He was a little one, maybe four feet long.

"Oh, he is Timmy, I guarantee," Justine said with a straight face. "I can tell by his smile, yes?"

Mrs. Lindstrom didn't react. I looked at her, noticing the dark circles under her careful eye make-up.

Justine called softly again. One by one, singly and in pairs, they came —Dolly, Henry, Azalea, Clinton, Marie, and Timmy again. "Dinner" was eagerly snapped from the pole in crushing jaws ringed by razor-sharp teeth.

"Oh, I can't believe it—I can't believe this isn't somebody else's dream and I just happen to be in it!" Burke breathed softly, leaning over the boat. "There are so *many* of them!"

"Not so many, today," Justine said. "This weather, the babies do not like it. They like sunshine, just like the snakes."

Burke pointed towards the water. "That one must be nearly ten feet long."

"A nice big bull, him," Justine said, watching Burke's hand. "Everybody—keep your hands *inside* the boat, yes?"

"Oh, darling, please, *please* be careful!" Mrs. Lindstrom said, looking pale. "If anything happened to those fingers . . ."

"I wish you'd think of something *original* to nag me about, Angelica!" Burke said angrily. "It's been *fingers* ever since I first picked up a toy violin! I mustn't play ball because I'd hurt my *fingers!* I mustn't *skate* because if I fell down I'd break my *fingers!* I mustn't ever *cook* because I might burn my *fingers!* I mustn't go swimming because the water would wrinkle my *fingers!*"

"There now, see?" Mrs. Lindstrom said tightly. "Your childish tantrum has frightened off the alligators. They're leaving." Several gently rippling wakes were moving towards the middle of the lake.

"They are also leaving," Justine said, grinning, "because there is no more chicken."

Burke turned around to face her. "Oh, let me call Timmy back! Isn't there even *one* little piece of meat left?"

"Oh, no, Burke, I do not think . . . ." She opened the plastic bag wide and looked in. "Oh, but here is one chunk, stuck to the bottom of the sack."

"Oh, good! Let me . . ." Burke started to stand.

Her mother said loudly, "Sit *down*, Burke! Of *course* you're not going to feed the alligators! You don't know anything about it! Don't let her, Justine!"

"Oh, no, you may not, Burke—it is Nonc's rule. Guests may *not* feed the alligators, them." Justine's voice was firm. She brushed raindrops off her face. "See, it is starting to rain, and I think it will be a big rain. We will go back to the boathouse now."

I couldn't get over it—my little cream puff the commander of an alligator expedition. I wondered how I'd feel, kissing an admiral. It could make a difference.

"Please, Justine," Burke pleaded. "I may never *ever* be here again! Just let me hold the pole after you put the meat on it!"

"Nonc says *no*, Burke. He trusts me, *chère*, to take good care of you." She laid the meat across the end of the pole. "Timmy? You are still here, Timmy?" She started to hold the pole out over the water.

"Oh, please, Justine—surely, just this once . . ." Quick as the lightning that was flashing in the east, Burke pushed between her mother and me and grabbed the pole.

"Sit *down*, Burke! Sit *down!*" Justine ordered, snatching the pole back.

"Burke! Oh, make her sit down, Maximilian! She'll fall in!" Mrs. Lindstrom turned and reached out for Burke, but

Burke pushed her mother's hands aside and was thrown off balance.

"Sit down, stupid!" I yelled at Burke, swinging around to grab her around the knees.

She screamed one short, piercing scream, flailing her arms, and twisting out of my grasp. Just before she hit the water I heard the familiar shriek, "You touched me!" It ended in a gurgle. I stared, immobile, horrified, at the spot where the water had closed over her. It was only slightly wind-riffled—as though Burke Lindstrom had never been.

"Burke!" Mrs. Lindstrom screamed. "Burke . . . oh, Burke . . ." The words ended in a whisper.

Once again I didn't think twice. *I'd* done it—panicked Burke. I'd have to go after her. I pulled off my deck shoes as Justine commanded, "Be calm. You, Maximilian, sit *down!* Everything will be fine." She tried to block me as I went overboard. I didn't know what she had in mind, but everything wasn't fine.

I hit bottom and opened my eyes, terrified that I might not find Burke, terrified that an alligator might find me. Then I saw her drifting upwards. She was easy to spot in that white outfit, maybe easy for 'gators, too. We bobbed to the surface together and she grabbed me around the neck—a stranglehold. I gasped for air and sucked in some before we went down, struggling together. Underwater, I broke her hold, clamping both of her wrists in one hand, my lungs close to bursting. We surfaced, and I grabbed her before she could grab me, hooking her head under my right arm, towing her backwards as I stroked with my left arm. She was kicking, and screaming and coughing, and I knew that my back was going to be raw from her finger-nails raking it, despite my shirt.

"Be calm! Do not kick! You are *fine,* Burke! Do not

scream! Over here, Maximilian.'' Through eyes that felt bloodshot, I saw Justine holding the pole over the water, *away* from us. Alligator lure? There *had* to be some around. I thought with sudden admiration that she hadn't tried to poke the pole at *me*—to pull me in. I'd have grabbed it through sheer instinct—and pulled *her* in. The boat was slowly circling us, quietly drawing nearer.

The rain pelted down, and thunder rolled over the lake. A flash of lightning illuminated something moving towards us—fast.

"Over here, Maximilian. Be calm. You are safe. I am working Timmy away from you. Keep coming, Maximilian.'' Her voice was low and soothing. I followed the sound—and brushed against something rough and scaly. My flesh crawled. I turned and looked into the smiling jaws of an alligator six feet away.

At that moment there was a *thwack* that sent a screen of water between him and me—and the jaws disappeared. It happened four more times before I reached the boat. Thanks to a good adrenalin rush, I heaved Burke up over the side, and hands hauled her in. I did the best push-up of my life, fell into the boat, and reeled in my feet. When I turned to look into the water, a half-submerged log with gimlet eyes looked back.

It took me a minute to get control of my chattering teeth. "Thanks, Justine,'' I gasped. I turned and looked at her through clear eyes. "You're—quite a girl.'' The skiff was heading across the lake.

Burke lay limply across the seat. I took her in my arms. Her mother hadn't moved. She looked traumatized. "Come on, Burke. You're okay now. You're okay.'' I brushed the stringy red hair back from her wet, blue-white face. Her eyes were closed. Was she . . . then I felt her heart beat-

ing, faintly, against my chest. "Got a poncho?" I said to
Justine. "She's cold." I wrapped myself around her,
shaking. We couldn't lose the ballgame now.

"No," Justine said. "I threw them all at the 'gators. I
knew they would think orange plastic might be good to eat,
them. They grabbed up the ponchos and swam away. You
are wanting to go back in, *cher*—to save the ponchos?"
She laughed lightly, but I saw her face. She was wearing
clown-white with big eyes drawn in black greasepaint. She
looked straight at me, into my eyes. "I am thinking, *cher* —
you are—quite a guy, hahn?"

If the scream-theme was pure horror, the ending was
pure fantasy: Burke's arms crept around my neck. She
seemed to be trying to say something. I put my face next
to hers—her lips brushed my cheek. They were ice cold.
"Hold me," she whispered. I held her all the way to the
dock.

On the road back to Houma in the car, the dam broke.
There was rain outside, and there was rain inside. Mrs.
Lindstrom pulled off the road and stopped the car. The ice
sculpture melted. She had started to cry. She cried with
big, wracking, shaking sobs, for maybe ten minutes. Burke
sat rigid and silent. Justine and I stared at each other, helpless. Then I saw Burke turn and reach out to her mom.
They held one another, while Justine and I listened to the
rain. I thought I was going to drown all over again—in
tears.

—*Whatever has happened, Burke, has made you more radiant than ever, a more brilliant performer. I have just learned that your next solo appearance will be at Lincoln Center with the New York Philharmonic. You are pleased about that, I should imagine.*

—*Yes, very. And I certainly won't have to travel far to keep my engagement, Mr. Aaronson.*

—*Dare I ask my charming but secretive guest what that means? You are a Californian, I believe.*

—*Until June. I am applying to the Juilliard School of Music and will be auditioning there this summer. So you see, I'll be right across the street from Lincoln Center*—*if I'm accepted.*

—*Do you really think there's a doubt? As you know, Burke, the conservatory has been my personal choice for you for some time. Do you regret this past semester's detour around your professional goal?*

—*Not at all. I've made some wonderful friends and have proved to my own satisfaction that I can't scatter my shots. Music requires total dedication.*

—*One more important question, Burke*—*and I think you know what it is.*

—*It no doubt concerns my second encore, Mr. Aaronson.*

—*That is a very enigmatic smile I see*—*rather like the Mona Lisa. But I'm going to ask the question anyway. Who is the "someone special" to whom you dedicated the dazzling, but thoroughly unexpected and unaccompanied Bach Praeludium in E Major?*

—*I'm afraid you*—*and our viewers*—*must be satisfied with what you call a*—*Mona Lisa smile.*

—*Does this "someone special" know it is for him*—*or her?*

—Oh, yes. I'm sure.

—And that must satisfy us for the present. Thank you, Burke. I have been talking with the very talented young violin virtuoso, Miss Burke Lindstrom, who has bedazzled the entire music world tonight with her masterful interpretation of Sibelius' D Minor Concerto for Violin, followed by the programmed encore, the lively Zapateado by Sarasate—and the impromptu Bach Praeludium to which she brought new emotional depth as well as a new brilliance. The sixteen-year-old Miss Lindstrom performed with the Houston Symphony Orchestra under the baton of guest conductor Daniel Sarazenski. Now back to our studios, from Jones Hall, in Houston.

★ ★ 18

"Hey," I said to Justine. "The TV show's over. I think we're supposed to congratulate Burke now, aren't we?" We were standing on the stage with what looked like a hundred other people, behind the closed curtain. I had tight hold of her hand—I didn't want to lose her in this melee. "Uh, who do you think 'someone special' is, Cherie?" I *knew* it was me—I was just testing her.

"Me." She smiled impishly. "I am her favorite friend, me."

"You're *my* favorite friend, anyhow." I didn't believe her, of course. "Did I tell you you are exotic and gorgeous and I'm groveling at your beautiful sandaled feet tonight, Raquel Welch?" She was wearing a long, fluffy white skirt and an off-the-shoulder blouse that showed off a lot of her—er, tan, especially since she had braided and pinned up her long hair in big sophisticated coils over each ear.

"You couldn't guess, Maximilian, yes? Burke *gave* me these things, *cher*. She says she has too much white. The skirt, it is fine, but the blouse, I think it is too small, yes?"

"Yes, I definitely think so. It's perfect. Don't change a thing. I happen to like the poured-in look." My eyes were devouring her, as they say.

"Maximilian, do you like *Burke's* dress tonight?"

"Pretty bad," I said promptly. "She's not the long slinky type. She's the long skinny type, and she should have picked something—fluffy. But *orange,* Cherie! I'd be the last pot to call the kettle black, as Dad puts it—but she looks like a lick of flame."

"Her maman let her choose anything she wanted. She wanted a nice bright color. Me, I gave Burke a present too, from Houma. A T-shirt. It is pink and it says, in white letters, '*Écrevisse.*' That means *crawfish.* And there is a little white crawfish on each sleeve."

She looked pretty self-satisfied with her taste in T-shirts, but I was appalled. *"Crawfish?* You gave her a T that says *crawfish,* Cherie? Do you think she'll consider that—er, flattering?"

"But yes! *Écrevisse*—it is also a symbol for us Cajuns, Maximilian. I have made Burke an Honorary Cajun, her!"

"What about me? Don't I get to be a crawfish, too?"

"It is different with you, *cher!* You have to *marry* a Cajun to be a Cajun!" She smiled that wide, pearly smile and I thought to myself, there are *worse* fates, Maximilian, you lucky *écrevisse!* Just hang in there for a few more years! A few more years? A lifetime! We'd be middle-aged.

"Maximilian! Justine!" Burke rushed up to us, trailing people and almost tripping on the long orange skirt again. She hugged Justine, and whispered in her ear. Then her arms were around *my* neck, and I found myself cautiously putting mine around her waist. But it was a weird feeling. I almost missed the familiar yell, "You touched me!"

"Maximilian," she whispered, "you are someone *very special* to me." It blew my mind. She really *had* played the last number—just for me. I guess I knew it all along.

"Thanks, Burke," I said, trying to sound cool. "You played—just great."

She pulled back and looked at me, her eyes shining. "I'll never forget you."

"Hey, no need to! We can write, can't we? Anyway, there's all the rest of this semester!" *She* was the special one. She was *really* someone special—a genuine genius, a weird girl, a special kind of—friend.

The newspaper people with their note pads and the photographers with their bulging gadget bags and cameras and the hangers-on like us caught up with her again, and we backed off.

"What did she say to you, Maximilian?" my Louisiana lovely asked curiously.

"Probably the same thing she said to you." It was a clever answer, I thought.

"To me, she said, 'Thank you for coming, Justine. You are a dear friend,' she said, her." Justine smiled knowingly.

"Same difference," I grinned. Who was I to spoil her day?

"You are weaseling, you," she said, her eyebrows coming together in a frown. "Maybe I will *really* put the gris-gris on you this time, if you are not nice, Maximilian."

"So you didn't trash the fingernail parings and lock of hair and that disgusting flat frog, after all! You have passed me another hot potato, Cherie." I put an arm around her waist.

Her eyes were laughing. "You do not believe all that stuff, Maximilian, yes?"

"Of course I believe it, you witch. I've been under your

spell from the moment we met. What are you planning to do to me this time?'' I pulled her close—as close as is proper with a Sophisticated Lady.

"Gris-gris is for bad things, *cher*. I was only fooling with you, Maximilian, me.'' Her Wicked Witch of the West smile was working its spell—my insides were turning squishy like Mississippi Mud Cake.

"Well, keep on fooling with me and you're headed for trouble, Miss Broomstick.'' I kissed her.

She pulled back, laughing. "Oh, Maximilian, not in front of *all* these people . . .'' I saw her eyes dart to the side of the stage. "Oh! There is Lanny, and his parents!'' There were also Burke's parents, standing near them— holding hands.

"He'd be the first to cheer us on,'' I said, grinning.

We were all staying at the posh Lone Star Lodge, and it wasn't costing Justine or me a cent. The Lindstroms were springing for the tab. "It's the *least* we can do,'' Mrs. Lindstrom had said emotionally, taking both my hands, as we said goodbye in the rain at the Landrys', after the big alligator jamboree.

"Burke and her maman came right to Houston, *cher*, did you know that? They stayed overnight in New Orleans and then flew here, and Burke, she says it has been lovely! She has been suntanning by the pool, and eating without even hunting for cockroaches, and practicing in the suite when she feels like it!'' My cute Cajun's cheeks were pink with the pleasure of disclosure.

"You sure got the scoop, Cherie. Good thing we bugged their suite with *you*.'' Mr. Lindstrom had moved out of it when Justine moved in, and was sharing a room with me. We had queen-size beds with gold spreads and a gold john.

It was the ultimate. "But that's not a suntan Burke has—that's contiguous freckles. I'd recognize them anywhere, even under all that make-up."

Justine laughed, grabbing my arm and hugging it. "You, Maximilian! I do *not* want you to leave so early tomorrow, *cher!* Why you cannot miss just one Inner-City Show?"

"Hello, you two!" Lanny appeared right next to us, smiling appreciatively at Justine. "You must have pull! I saw you in the best seats in the house—fifth row center."

I grinned. "I dig this up-scale life style. I could get used to it."

"Then make sure you catch the grand finale, the supper tonight. My parents are pulling out all the stops." It happened to be at the top of our postconcert agenda, but I had already decided to skip the truffles this time around—*and* the champagne.

"Lanny, there you are!" Burke had escaped her claque—I noticed the crowd had thinned out. She was holding one of the big bouquets, wrapped in cellophane, that I had seen piled around on tables and chairs, armloads of flowers that were given to her when she took her bows.

"The roses are *beautiful*, Lanny!" They were orange, a perfect match for a lick of flame.

"No more so than you, love." He didn't make a move to touch her, but his eyes had that hungry look that matched the way I felt when I looked at Justine.

A glow was spreading over Burke's face, maybe because it *was* warm on the stage, behind the curtain. "You and Ann and Raoul are always so . . ."

"Read the card, darling. The roses are from plain old *me*. Mother and Dad are old enough now to shift for themselves, and I'm sure they have something more than roses in mind." He sounded jaunty, but he looked—well, wistful. I think Burke picked up on that.

"But the roses are *all* that I want! They are so—perfect!" She was smiling.

He said, "Oh, I nearly forgot. I have something else for you."

There was a lot of the old fear in her voice when she said, "Lanny, *no! Don't* spoil it!"

He took a little tissue-wrapped object from his pocket and handed it to her. "It's a genuine handcarved Looft— for the dedicated carousel-collector."

She looked at him questioningly. "If you mean the great merry-go-round carver, that's Charles *Looff,* and I don't understand . . ." She unwrapped it. We moved in for a closer look. It was a primitive little wooden horse about an inch high, with gaily painted trappings.

"It *is* a genuine Looft," Lanny said solemnly. "Jerry Looft. He has a sidewalk stand on Telegraph Avenue in Berkeley."

Burke looked dismayed, then she started breaking up. I had never seen her laugh like that before. She laid the flowers down on a chair, and reached out towards Lanny. He took her hands in his. She looked up at him, still laughing, and Justine and I moved discreetly away. All *we* had to give Burke was her own space. I glanced at my pink and white rose as she clutched my arm, smiling. To each his own, as they say.

Creel, Chihuahua, Mex.
July 6

Dear Max,

My friend, I have news! At last I have the student visa, and I will be coming back to Belview Beach in September! I am happy that you and your parents want me to live at your house. I will like that very much, and it will give me a fine chance to whip you into shape for the next Kola King Marathon. But I am afraid you will not win until Justine goes away to some other place. I am glad to hear Burke has already moved to New York—that is one less woman to worry about. But it is bad news that you are now skating with Trinka on some Saturday mornings when Justine is busy with her summer school homework. I beg you to give up this skating, Max.

I like your letters, and I am very interested in your new job, helping the damaged children. The pay is plenty good too, even though you have to give half of it to your papa every payday to pay for the yellow VW Bug he got you. I think that he is a very happy man that you want to take some child psychology classes in college.

Well, you did not need your old job back at the gas station, Max, so it does not matter that you couldn't get it back anyway. I will get back my old job at Paco's. Paco, he needs us legal aliens that speak good English and are not afraid of the INS. Soon I will give you back your money, Max, even if you don't want it, like you said. Then you can start your old-magazine collection again, but I *think your mama is right, now you are rid of a big fire hazard, and you are $50 U.S. ahead.*

Don't worry that you are not up in lights at the Music Center like Burke was and like you think Justine will be someday. Max, why are you thinking you have to know who you are IN LIGHTS? What you are is a friend, and that job you do better than anyone else, my friend.

Mama says please give her respectful regards to your fine parents.

Adios, your friend,
Roberto el Conejo (the Rabbit)

*VERY BEST THANKS
FROM THE AUTHOR AND*

*BURKE, to
Barbara Simons Transue, Dorothy Wade,
and Michael Sushel: professional musicians*

*MAXIMILIAN, to
Linda Lee: professional mime*

*MAXIMILIAN AND THE RABBIT, to
Ed Grace and Bill Hayden: marathoners*

*JUSTINE, to
Diane Glasgow, Cherie Eckert, and
the friendly Cajuns of Louisiana
from Houma to Mamou*

*LANNY, to
Ken Grace: entomologist*

*EVERYBODY, to
Sonia Levitin*

*for
A VERY PRIVATE PERFORMANCE*